THE NEPHITE CHRONICLES

CAPSTONE OF FAITH

ROBERT H. MOSS

COPYRIGHT © 1995 BY Robert H. Moss Second Edition
First Edition 1984

All Rights Reserved

No part of this book may be reproduced in any form whatsoever, whether by graphic, visual, electronic, filming, microfilming, tape recording, or any other means, without prior written permission of the author, except in the case of brief passages embodied in critical reviews and articles.

This book is not an official publication of the Church of Jesus Christ of Latter-day Saints. All opinions expressed herein are the author's and are not necessarily those of the publisher's or of the Church of Jesus Christ of Latter-day Saints.

ISBN: 1-55517-200-8

1 2 3 4 5 6 7 8 9 10

Published by:
Acme Publishers, 1795 Ann Dell Lane, Salt Lake City, UT 84121

Printed and Distributed in the United States of America by:

925 North Main, Springville, Ut 84663 801-489-4084

Cover Design by Lyle Mortimer
Typeset by Stephen J. Bons

OTHER BOOKS BY ROBERT H. MOSS

THE NEPHITE CHRONICLES
Covenant Coat—A Novel of Joseph
I Nephi—A Novel of Nephi and His Family
Waters of Mormon—A Novel of Alma, The Elder
That I Were An Angel—A Novel of Alma, The Younger
Title of Liberty— A Novel of Moroni and Helaman
The Abridger—A Novel of Mormon
Valiant Witness—A Novel of Moroni
Capstone of Faith—Gaining A Testimony of the Book of Mormon

Celestial Child, A Biography of a Downs-Syndrome Child
A Readers' Doctrinal Digest of the Book of Mormon
A Readers' Doctrinal Digest of the Old Testament
The Moss Family—1837-1993

ABOUT THE AUTHOR

Robert H. Moss was born in the little Swess community of Santa Clara, Utah. He graduated fromDixie College in St. George, Utah, where he studied under several talented authors and through them he developed a love for history and a desire to write.

Following college he entered the US Army, and served on several bases in the United States and Germany. After his discharge he finished his studies at the College of Southern Utah and Brigham Young University. He taught elementary school for five years, was an elementary school principal, and became a superintendent of schools. Upon completion of his doctorate in educational administration at BYU, he became a college professor, teaching at the University of Northern Colorado and Southern Utah State College.

His church service has included callings as bishop, bishop's counselor, Young men's president, stake missionary, Seventy's Quarum president, Sunday School teacher, and temple ordinance worker.

He is an active person and enjoys parachuting, backpacking, rappelling, survival training, and other outdoor activities. Robert and his wife, Roberta, have five sons and several grandchildren. They reside in Salt Lake City, Utah.

Contents

Foreword ix
Chapter One 1
Chapter Two 11
Chapter Three 21
Chapter Four 35
Chapter Five 45
Chapter Six 59
Chapter Seven 69
Chapter Eight 79
Chapter Nine 89
Chapter Ten 97
Chapter Eleven 107
Chapter Twelve 115
Chapter Thirteen 127
Chapter Fourteen 135
Chapter Fifteen 147
Chapter Sixteen 155
Afterward 163

Forward

The Nephite Chronicles books focus on the heroes of the Book of Mormon. Books include novels of Joseph, Nephi, Alma, Alma the Younger, The Sons of Mosiah, General Moroni, Helaman, Mormon, and Moroni. By precept and example, each of these prophets taught much about life and living.

This final book of the series, Capstone of Faith, takes a different perspective. Instead of focusing on a particular hero in the Book of Mormon, the focus is on a person—a person just like you and me—who through right choices, develops hero characteristics; not necessarily those characteristics that make a person a hero in battle, but those traits of moral courage, forgiveness, honesty, and integrity that win the battles of daily living.

Each of us is a hero in embryo. Napoleon said each of his soldiers carried a "marshall's baton," ie, each had the capability of leadership. Every person has the capacity and capability to become a hero.

At some point in life, each must come to grips with those things of paramount concern in our lives: family, religion, and even more basic, who we are and what we are. Our self-image, the picture we hold of ourselves, plays an important part in any change, any growth, or any relationship.

Paul Dunn, in his book Dimensions of Life, says that "Life has many dimensions. It is full of challenges and joys. The abundant life can best be achieved through the practical application of true gospel principles." That is the focus of this book, to see what choices are available within Gospel principles, how they are made, and what the ultimate consequences of those choices might be.

This book is not the boy meets girl, boy falls in love with girl, boy marries girl type of love story. Of course, that is a predictable part of the story, because that is life. The real emphasis of this book is looking at a person who seeks truth and finds it.

I hope you have enjoyed each book in the Nephite Chronicles series and that this book, Capstone of Faith, will represent a gestalt for you in your own life as you seek for truth.

Chapter 1

Sal shivered involuntarily, struggled to his knees, and groped in the darkness until he felt the cool roundness of the toilet. Nausea hit him again. He hugged the porcelain fixture, his burning throat contracting in convulsive spasms. Hammers of pain beat against his temples, forcing a low groan from his lips. Slowly he stood and flipped the shower light. Though dim, its brightness increased the throbbing.

"Why?" Sal asked himself as he looked at his pale image in the mirror. Liquid, black expressionless eyes stared back at him. They were not accusing nor even sympathetic. "I know better," he said softly, his voice filled with despair. "I don't even like to drink." He leaned over the sink and splashed tepid water in his face. "What would Amy think?"

Several times Amy had told him he was good-looking. Now as he looked at his reflection in the mirror he couldn't understand why. Since his youth he had been ashamed of his olive complexion. Now his rounded face with its remains of teen-age pimples increased his feeling of self-disgust. Even high cheekbones inherited from Indian ancestors failed to impress him. His eyes showed no whites—even when he felt good the whites of his eyes were cream-colored. Now, black irises faded into a brownish-pinkish mass, all framed by heavy, black lashes.

Brushing his teeth vigorously failed to rid his mouth of the bitter taste of bile, heavy on his tongue. He dropped the lid on the toilet—the sound bouncing off the tile walls of the small bathroom—and sat down, his face cushioned in his hands. Sobs began deep in his chest and erupted from his mouth. Tears welled in his eyes and spilled through latticed fingers. He dropped to the floor on his knees, elbows on the toilet lid, hands clasped tightly together. "Mother of God," he prayed. "Help me." He lapsed into silence, unsure of his words. The need to pray existed. Actually uttering the words of prayer embarrassed him. Besides, he remained unsure that God listened, especially to him. Nagging deeper in his reasoning was a question. Is there a God— let alone one who listens?

He thought of his home—of his humble mother with her icons scattered throughout the small apartment they called home—in the heat and dryness of New Mexico. She had been so thrilled when he received the tennis scholarship. Her excitement cooled when friends told her Brigham Young University was a "Mormon" school.

"Salvador," she had pleaded. "No Se va!—Don't go."

"Don't worry," Sal had told her. "I will be a good Catholic and attend mass."

That seemed to reassure her. His three younger sisters presented a different problem. "Going to be a Mormon and have many wives," they teased.

He felt guilty about the lie he told his mother. Since coming to BYU he had made no effort to attend mass or be a practicing Catholic. The closest he came to any religious worship was the Saint Christopher medal he used to hang from his car mirror—when he had a car. He smiled—more of a grimace. His mother's small cluttered apartment would fit in Amy's living room. Even all of his father's keepsakes—knives, an old sword, a few dusty books, and several unworkable pistols— would fit with room to spare.

He still marveled at the size of Amy's huge house. That comes from having a dentist for a father, he thought with envy. What had his father been? A seasonal crop worker, a coal miner. More and more he found himself envying the gringoes and being ashamed of his own meager upbringing. They have everything and I have nothing, he thought.

Sal had been four when his father died in a mine cave-in. His mother had told him often how proud his father had been of his heritage—both Spanish and Indian. Sal tried to picture the man who had sacrificed to provide shelter and food for the family. Nothing came but images of wizened faces of Mexican men he had known as a youth. He felt none of the pride of which his mother spoke; only the shame of being poor, being different, and being Hispanic.

He had done fairly well in school. Somehow his mother's urgings had given him ambition to strive for good grades and excellence in athletics. Now he lived in the gringo town of Provo, Utah, attending a gringo college, in love with a gringo girl, and competing on a gringo tennis court.

The insistent ringing of the front doorbell interrupted his reverie. He winced, wondering who could be here so early in the morning. He glanced at his wristwatch with surprise—11:30; no longer early.

His roommates, Jose and Enrique, were out of town. He splashed cold water on his face, patted down his hair, and slipped on his robe as he walked to the door. Through the window he saw Amy. Oh, no, he thought. I can't let her see me like this. Returning to the bathroom, he wet his hair and slicked it down, then again splashed cold water on his face, hoping to rid himself of the dark bags under his eyes. The doorbell sounded again.

"Coming," he called, wincing at his croaky voice. He dropped the robe and pulled a t-shirt over his head, being careful not to mess his hair. He slipped on a pair of faded blue jeans and stepped into his sneakers. Without tying them, he headed again for the door.

Amy stood there, bright as sunshine, dressed in white tennis togs. A lovely smile revealed glowing teeth and crinkled her eyes the way he loved so much. "Sal," she said. "I've been calling all morning. This is the first nice weather we've had since the snow melted. You said you wanted a game of tennis before noon."

He tried to smile brightly, but was afraid his effort looked mediocre at best. "I took the phone and pecked her on the cheek. "I'll get my clothes." He turned back into the apartment and called back over his shoulder. "Come in and make yourself comfortable."

In the bathroom he scrubbed his face again, slipped into tennis clothes, and grabbed his racket and a can of balls from the closet.

"Whap!"

Sal drove the ball across the net, a clean serve into Amy's court.

With both hands grasping the racquet, Amy returned the volley. The ball went back and forth until Sal killed it into the net. "Set point," Amy called.

Frustrated, Sal hit doubles—both serves long—into the add court. He tossed his racquet into the air in disgust. It bounced on the hard court. As he leaned over to pick it up Amy came up to him with a smile. "Poor loser," she chuckled.

Sal growled some unintelligible response. He grabbed a towel from the end post and swiped it across his sweating face. He looked at Amy. She sat on the bench, pulling a light, white sweater over her tennis outfit. He marveled again at her beauty. Short, blond hair barely brushed freckled shoulders. Sweat darkened the fringes above her temples. Her clear skin, with its natural blush on high cheekbones—enhanced now by physical activity—contrasted sharply with his own dark skin. He loved the freckles dotting her nose. I'm in love with her, he thought, but what does she see in me?

She patted the bench beside her. He sat and took her hand.

"Thanks for the exercise, Sal." She sat for a few moments, just holding his hand, then swiveled on the bench and looked seriously at him.

He looked down.

She put her hand under his chin and raised it so she could look into his eyes. "Sal, I asked the Elders to come over and give you the missionary discussions. Did they show up?"

He shifted his feet uncomfortably and looked again at the ground. "They called."

"Called?"

"I had too much homework. I told 'em not to come."

Amy looked quickly away, hiding tears that formed in her eyes. "Sal, I thought you said you cared about me."

"I do, very much," Sal said, squeezing her hand.

"If you don't care enough to at least listen to what the Elders have to say, then you really don't care."

"That is not true," he said quickly. "I just don't see that studying religion has anything to do with you and me."

"It has everything to do with us," she said quietly. "My family and my religion are my life. I can't have one without the other. I've told you before the man I marry must be worthy to take me to the temple."

Sal turned and stared at snow-capped Timpanogas. "Why?"

"Why?" she said, suddenly angry. "Why! Because when I marry I will marry someone who will love me forever, not just for this short life." She stood and picked up her sports bag. "And if you're not willing to make that kind of commitment, then I guess you're not the man for me." She stormed off the court, leaving the wire gate swinging.

Sal looked at her retreating back with misery in his eyes. He wanted nothing more than to please Amy, but at that he had proven to be a miserable failure. A similar spat the previous evening had triggered last night's drinking. Just the thought of it brought back the rotten taste.

Pah! He slung his jacket over his shoulder, picked up his bag, and slowly followed her.

The ride back to the apartment was tense and silent. Riding with Amy in her red Grand Prix was usually fun. Sal tried to think of something to say, but could not. Instead, he just sat there feeling miserable. Amy dropped him off and drove off without a word.

He slammed the door and stood behind it. His apartment was a mess. He threw his bag on the floor, opened the door of the refrigerator and stared at the contents for a few moments, then shut it without getting anything. He really did not feel like eating. He walked over to the couch and picked up the Book of Mormon Amy had given him. The Book of Mormon, A New Witness For Christ. He leafed through the preface and testimonies without paying any attention. "I, Nephi,"... he read. He skimmed through two chapters, grimacing as verse after verse repeated the trite phrase, "And it came to pass; and it came to pass." He put the book down and walked again to the refrigerator. "And it came to pass," he said aloud as he grabbed some baloney, Miracle Whip, and mustard. "And it came to pass that my life is a total failure," he chanted as he slapped Miracle Whip and mustard on the bread.

Returning to the couch, he struggled through the next few chapters. The part about Nephi killing Laban disturbed him, but he read on through the rest of First Nephi, understanding little of what he read. Dropping the book on the coffee table, he picked up his text for medieval history, flipped through a few pages then set it down. He could not concentrate. He flipped on the TV and watched the end of a sitcom rerun. The phone rang. "Sal," Amy said. "I'm sorry I got upset."

"It was my fault," Sal said. "By the way," he chuckled, "I just finished First Nephi."

There was a pause on the telephone—almost as if she had not believed him. Then she spoke up enthusiastically. "That's wonderful!" she said. "It's a great story."

"I guess I need you to explain it to me," Sal said. "I really didn't feel like I understood it."

"I'd love to."

"When can you come over?"

"What about Jose and Enrique?"

"They won't be back 'til Monday."

"Have you had lunch?"

"I fixed me a baloney sandwich."

"I'll bring something to eat and be over about four."

Sitting close beside Amy thrilled him. He put his arm around her shoulders and pulled her to him.

"No, Sal," she said. But she did not make him remove his arm. His thoughts were so much on Amy, and her closeness, that she had to keep reminding him they were studying. With her beside him, the first part of the Book of Mormon was easy enough—a family's journey from Jerusalem into the desert—except for the slaying of Laban.

"Why did Nephi have to kill him?" Sal asked. "I thought God gave a commandment that 'Thou shalt not kill.'"

"Nephi killed Laban to get the brass plates."

"Why were they so important?"

Amy was patient. "The brass plates contained their scriptures—much of what we know now as the Old Testament."

"But to kill a man ..."

"I guess I don't understand all of the reasons," Amy said, "but when the Lord commands us to do something we have to obey, even if we don't want to. That's all Nephi did. He obeyed God."

"You actually think God talks to people?" Sal asked, a little flippantly.

Amy looked at him intently, her blue eyes gazing into his black ones, before he dropped them.

"On that one concept lies our entire cause for existing as a church. Without it there wouldn't be a Mormon Church—we would be like all the others."

Sal decided to drop that point. "So they crossed the ocean and landed in America?"

"Probably in Central America," Amy answered.

"And I suppose you even know where?" Sal was cynical.

Amy waited several moments before she spoke, trying hard to be patient—though her student didn't seem to want to learn. "I don't know, Sal. Archaeologists here at BYU have proposed several theories."

"Oh?" There was still cynicism in his voice.

She shrugged. "I really don't suppose it matters. Either the Book of Mormon is true, or it isn't. The archeological evidence helps, but the book has to stand on its own merits."

"You've told me you know it's true."

"With all my heart."

"How do you know? How does anyone know?"

"Let me show you what Moroni says." She started flipping through the book.

"You've read that before," Sal said tiredly. "How else could I find out for myself if it is true?"

"I don't know," Amy said sadly. "The only sure way is for the Holy Ghost to witness to you."

"Which means?"

"Which means you must read it and pray about it," she tried to reason. "It's not like your history book." She picked up the medieval history. "These books are authors' opinions or interpretations. They rely on words of others. The Book of Mormon came directly from God to man. You must prove its truthfulness by the witness of the Spirit."

Sal stood up and walked to the refrigerator. "Let's eat. I'm starved." He grabbed the tray of enchiladas Amy had brought and started for the microwave.

Amy was almost in tears. She ate in silence, not even looking at him.

When they finished eating, Sal took her hand. "Amy,

I'll really try to read and understand the Book of Mormon"

"To really understand it will take more than reading," Amy said stubbornly, "you'll have to pray about it."

After Amy left, Sal dropped to his knees. He was still unsure about praying, but managed to say, "God, this book is important to Amy, so I've got to read it. Please help me. I need to understand it."

Chapter 2

The line of students extended almost a block inside the massive Smith Fieldhouse. Amy clasped Sal's hand. "I'm convinced if I can make it through registration, I can make it through college," she punctuated her words with a short laugh.

"I hate lines," Sal replied sullenly. "College wouldn't be half-bad if I didn't have to stand in stupid lines."

Amy held up her packet. "Have you made out your class schedule?"

"I've written down some classes I want, but classes fill so fast, I don't know if I'll get any of them."

Amy looked around the room.

Sal continued, unabated. "Besides, last semester's grades were so bad I'm on academic probation. I need to take some easy classes this semester so I can bring up my GPA."

"Are you still planning to major in history?"

"When I get around to declaring a major," Sal said, looking at his class list. "I still have some general ed groups to fill." He added dryly, "The only class I'm sure of getting is tennis."

"What about religion?" Amy asked, looking at him quizzically.

"Ya." Sal's laconic response lacked any vestige of enthusiasm. "Last semester I took Comparative Christian Religions. I'll find something."

"Why not work your schedule so you can take Book of Mormon with me," she said brightly. "I'm signed up for

Brother Moody's Tuesday-Thursday class." Amy waved at someone in the other line.

"Who was that?" "Just a fellow."

Sal felt a pang of jealousy. He looked where Amy had waved. With relief he noted they were getting close to the registration tables.

"Well?" Amy said.

Sal detected a small note of irritation in her voice. "Well, what?" he asked.

"I asked you about taking a Book of Mormon class with me," Amy sounded a little exasperated. "Do you want to or not?"

"Sure, sure," Sal said, pulling out his class schedule. "Where is it?"

"Under religion, silly," she said. "Brother Moody's class, section 17."

Sal checked to make sure the class fit his schedule, then penciled it in. By now they were at the registration desk. Sal politely waited for Amy, then handed his packet to the woman behind the table. She scanned through his class list. "I'm sorry. All Botany sections are filled. Are there any other science classes you want to take this semester?"

"I needed botany to fill my biological science group."

"Do you have your social sciences filled?"

"Not yet."

"There is an archaeology class open. It's taught at the same time as the botany class. It will count on your social sciences."

"Okay," Sal grumbled. "Archaeology, yuck. It even sounds hard." He caught Amy's frown and changed his demeanor to a smile. "I don't even know how to spell it," he said quickly.

The first week flew by and Sal settled into the routine of class work.

The first day of Book of Mormon class Brother Moody started out with a joke about his teaching methods: "The definition of a lecture is numb on one end and dumb on the other." He waited for the ripple of polite laughter to end, then continued. "We will use the Book of Mormon as our text. Since I don't believe in lecturing, we will read and study it together. Each day you will turn in a one-page paper dealing with a particular subject found in the Book of Mormon"

Sal shrugged. That sounded easy enough. Then Brother Moody went into a long lecture—Sal nudged Amy and winked—about the importance of the Book of Mormon Then he said something that really caught Sal's attention. "A benefit of scripture often overlooked is the role of prophets as models. The Book of Mormon prophets are my heroes."

Someone in front, a tall man, raised his hand. "What do you call heroes?"

Brother Moody answered. "By a hero, I mean someone I look to as a model, or we might even say a mentor."

Brother Moody's next statement really intrigued him. "Most of us develop poor self-images somewhere along the way. Sterling Sill said 'having an inferiority complex is the universal disease- -everyone has it.' What helped most to improve my own self-image was to look at the lives of others. I picked out the positive characteristics they demonstrated."

He looked around, a shy smile playing on his lips. "I know you won't believe this, but when I was young I had a very poor self-image. I was shy and didn't think I was worth very much. One of the main ways I overcame low self-esteem was reading of the Book of Mormon and identifying those things which made each of the prophets great. Then I tried to apply those things to my life."

Sal took good notes as Brother Moody talked about each of the prophets. He left the class thinking carefully about what Brother Moody had said. *That's what I need, he thought. Someone to pattern my life after. Someone who can be a model for me.*

That night he and Amy discussed the reading assignment. Sal asked, "Why did Moody start talking about the Doctrine and Covenants? I thought we were studying the Book of Mormon."

Amy smiled. "Brother Moody quoted from the 20th Section of the D.&.C. which explained the coming forth of the Book of Mormon but verse nine is the important one."

Sal wanted to ask a question, but Amy was too intent on what she was saying.

"This verse says the Book of Mormon is a record of a fallen people and contains the fullness of the Gospel of Jesus Christ." She looked at Sal. "That's why it is so important to us." Her eyes teared up. "But Sal, the most important verses are verses 14 and 15."

Sal reached over and helped hold up the book. He found the verses and read them aloud:

"And those who receive it in faith, and work righteousness, shall receive a crown of eternal life; But those who harden their hearts in unbelief, and reject it, it shall turn to their own condemnation.

Amy put the book down and threw her arms around Sal's neck. "Oh, Sal," she cried. "Please try to understand and love the Book of Mormon as much as I do."

The second class period Brother Moody discussed the "Fullness of the Gospel." Sal faithfully took notes and really tried to understand what the class was talking about. Much of it seemed as dogmatic as the catechisms he had taken as a child in the Catholic Church. In class they analyzed Chapter 27 of Third Nephi. It described the elements of the Gospel as doing the will of the Father, faith, the atonement of the Savior, baptism, the laying on of hands for the gift of the Holy Ghost, and sanctification.

Shyly he raised his hand. "In the Catholic Church we also believe in sanctification. Isn't that the granting of sainthood?"

Brother Moody smiled. "That's one element of it. However, in the Mormon Church the Lord describes sanctification as making individuals holy or purified."

Sal had hoped to study the book from front cover to back. Brother Moody's style of jumping all over, studying one particular doctrine after another, confused him. Sal dogmatically began at the beginning and quickly gained an understanding of First Nephi. Without realizing it, he read without his previous skepticism. To him it was a good story, and like any well-written story he became involved in the plot. Soon he was into Lehi's farewell to his family in Second Nephi. Sal was impressed with the words of the old Patriarch. He recognized the logic of Lehi's explanation of the temptation in the garden of Eden. He tried to joke with Amy. "Okay," he said. "I believe this part is true." He read: *'If Adam had not transgressed, he would not have fallen.'* "That only makes good sense."

"But you need to read the next part. I think it is the most important," Amy said seriously. She read: *'...wherefore they would have remained in a state of innocence, having no joy, for they knew no misery; doing no good, for they knew no sin... Adam fell that men might be; and men are that they might have joy.'*

"What does that mean?"

"To me it means that we learn and grow through our experiences." Amy stared into the distance for a moment, then continued softly. "It also means we were placed here on the earth to be happy, but the only way we can be happy is to follow the Savior's teachings."

Sal turned back to the book, reading silently through the next few verses, then looked up at Amy, hoping she would understand his next question. "Amy," he began a little haltingly, "Brother Moody talked about using prophets as role models. I like Nephi and think I could use him as a model, especially his willingness to obey God." He laughed self-consciously, "Even if it meant killing Laban." Embarrassed, he doggedly continued. "The other thing I was impressed with was his loyalty to his parents. He stuck with his father, though Laman and Lemuel fought him."

"Let me tell you one other thing about Nephi." Amy spoke quietly. "Nephi was so spiritual that he talked with God, and God's Spirit talked to him."

Midterm examination time came. Sal did fairly well in all of his other classes, but he was worried about the Book of Mormon class. What kind of exam would Brother Moody give? He went to class expecting the worst. Amy was already there. She squeezed his hand. Brother Moody didn't have a stack of exams on his desk. That was one good sign. He was smiling. Sal wasn't sure whether that was a good sign or not.

"The midterm exam will be essay," Brother Moody said.

A groan went up from the class.

Brother Moody continued as if he hadn't heard. "There are only three questions." He turned and wrote on the board:

1. What are the contents of the Book of Mormon and how can I recognize its message to me?

2. What are the purposes of the Book of Mormon as revealed by the Lord?

3. Name some "hero" characteristics modeled by at least three Book of Mormon prophets you have studied.

Sal looked at Amy. She smiled her reassurance, then turned her concentration to her own paper. He had a sinking feeling in his stomach as he wrote, knowing he did not write what the teacher wanted. *#1. The Book of Mormon is the purported story of a group of people who settled in America prior to the time of Columbus. If the story is true, which I am not sure of at this time, they— along with those who came across the glacial land bridge between Siberia and Alaska about 12,000 years ago—*

became my ancestors, the Native Americans. By the time Columbus came to the Americas, there were probably about 90 million people already here. Some of those people could have descended from the family of Lehi.

He paused and looked at the board question again, then continued writing.

I don't know what message the book has for me. I am still trying to find that out. I don't even know if I will recognize that message if and when it comes.

#2. The Book of Mormon is an interesting book. I am not sure what purposes it might have. If it did in actuality come from the Lord, its purposes could include telling me about my ancestors, giving me guidelines and truths upon which I can base my life, and telling me of the goodness and mercy and greatness of God. The purpose the book itself gives is to convince people of the reality of Jesus Christ and his message.

Number three was easy for Sal. He and Amy had talked often of each of the prophets and their characteristics. *#3. Nephi: Obedience, loyalty to parents, spirituality. Alma the Elder: Willingness to listen, and although only one man, he was willing to act; repentance. Alma the Younger: Zealous in a cause (even if it was the wrong one to begin with). Captain Moroni: courageous; willing to stand for what was right; patriotic.*

Sal looked at his paper, glanced around at the other class members, bending studiously over exam notebooks—writing volumes. He put his name on the paper, stood, touched Amy on her shoulder as he walked by and then, without looking back, dropped the paper on Brother Moody's desk and walked from the room. He left, feeling he had blown the first two questions.

"Sal," the voice on the telephone said. "This is Brother Moody. Is it possible to see you today?"

"Sure."

He called Amy.

"Guess who called today?"

"Who?"

"Brother Moody," he said, "and it didn't come as a surprise."

"Why do you say that?"

"Since the midterm I've taken less interest in class."

"So I've noticed," she said drily. "And today is the day for posting midterm grades."

"I hate to look."

"What are your other classes like?"

"I think I did all right in archaeology. I'm glad I took it. Of all the classes, other than the Book of Mormon I enjoy it most."

Amy listened patiently, though she had little interest in archaeology.

"I found an entirely new way of looking at history—of mankind's feeble accomplishments." He spoke almost in awe. "Archaeology lays out a tapestry for people to inspect and learn from."

"What kind of grade will you get?"

"The course is introductory and strictly from the book. I think I'll get an 'A'."

Brother Moody, when Sal met him, drove straight to the point. "Sal, I appreciate your candor in your midterm. I don't expect you to have the same belief concerning the Book of Mormon as I expect from members of the Church. However, I can hold you to the same level of study and scholarship that I require of members."

When Brother Moody paused, Sal nodded, wondering when the "F" would fall.

Brother Moody continued. "You can look very objectively at the Book of Mormon Your study, if you want, can attempt to disprove the book. Or it can be a study of finding those things within the book's covers which justify it as reading material for non-LDS students. I want you to set up the criterion for your study, but I expect it to be scholarly."

Sal was taken back. "You mean you're not going to fail me because of my mid-term?"

A smile was the only response Brother Moody gave.

Sal was excited as he talked with Amy. "I've never had a professor treat me that way before," he said. "He gave me responsibility for my own learning."

"So what have you decided?" Amy asked.

"I want to tie my study of the Book of Mormon in with my study of archaeology," he spoke enthusiastically "You told me the only way I would know if the Book of Mormon was true was to read it and pray about it." He paced the narrow apartment excitedly as he talked. "But I feel I can prove it through the archaeological evidence the people of the Book of Mormon did or did not leave behind."

Amy drew back a little, almost frightened by his burst of enthusiasm. "What will you do?"

"I'll take Brother Moody's challenge and work on verifying the consistency of the Book of Mormon. Next year..." He paused. "Next year, I want to get some practical experience in archaeological research."

Chapter 3

Sal laid out as many premises as he felt he could research, starting with questions that had come to his mind when he first picked up the book: 1) The Bible is the whole word of God—God has spoken and speaks no more. 2) It seems the Book of Mormon contradicts the Bible. 3) If the Book of Mormon were true, it would be more popular. More people would be reading it and living by its teachings.

The BYU library had a big section of anti-Mormon literature. Sal looked through the books, many of which attempted to disprove the Book of Mormon He spent hours adding to his list of questions—things he had never thought about, such as: 1) The Book of Mormon is based on the Spaulding Manuscript—not on Joseph Smith's fantastic revelations; 2) It is difficult to accept that Jesus Christ appeared on the American continent after his resurrection in Jerusalem. Third Nephi only quotes from the King James Bible. 3) Horses and elephants were used by the Nephites. The books listed other challenges that he would have liked to have time to pursue: such things as houses being made cement and the Nephites using machinery and wheels when the archaeological evidence seemed to indicate otherwise.

He looked over his list, taking Professor Moody's challenge to heart. "My only concern," he told Amy, "is I am spending so much time for my Book of Mormon class that I'm neglecting my other classes."

"So what's your purpose?" Amy asked.

He took her hand. "Brother Moody suggested the best way for me to learn if the Book of Mormon is true, is to try to prove it false."

Amy drew back, aghast. "Sal, is that wise?"

He laughed. "Your professor is the one who suggested the study to me."

Sal carefully studied dozens of books which raised the issue of the Spaulding manuscript. That seemed to be the most oft-quoted denunciation of the Book of Mormon. When he thought he had prepared enough, he rehearsed in his mind how he would ask the question. In class he raised his hand. Brother Moody called on him.

"Brother Moody," Sal said, a little shyly. "I have reading many books about the Spaulding Manuscript. I have quotes from many people which state that Joseph Smith merely used this story to create a work of fiction."

"That's very interesting. What about it, class?" Brother Moody asked. "Does anyone have an answer for Sal?"

A girl in the front row—one that Sal felt was a teacher pleaser; always parroting back answers Brother Moody was looking for—raised her hand. When called on, she turned in her seat and looked directly at Sal. "Most scholars," the girl said—Sal remembered her name as being Lola— "have found the Book of Mormon could not have been written by one man. Many prophets contributed to the **Book of Mormon**." She turned back to the front—smugly, Sal thought.

"That seems to be just your opinion," Sal said, somewhat hotly.

"No," she said, without turning. "A team of linguistic scholars, using computers, tested the differences in writing between each of the books in the Book of Mormon and concluded the writing was that of many different people."

Brother Moody asked, "Does anyone else wish to take up this line of reasoning?"

A returned missionary behind Sal, Rod was his name, raised his hand. "I really don't think it is something we need to discuss," he said. "The only way to find if the *Book of Mormon* is true is to follow the procedure found in Moroni 10 and let the Holy Ghost bear witness."

Sal smiled. He had figured in advance that would be the ultimate cop-out.

Brother Moody surprised him. "That's extremely important for you and me, Rod. But at this point Sal needs an answer based on evidence and logic rather than spiritual manifestation."

A student in the back row—one who had never taken part in class discussion—timidly raised his hand. Sal turned to look at him, a person he had hardly noticed in class. The boy's horn- rimmed glasses dominated his too-small face and he was so short he barely came above the desk.

"Professor Moody," the boy began, "the Spaulding manuscript has been examined by hosts of Mormon and Non-Mormon scholars. All of them, without exception, have come to the conclusion that there is no relationship between it and the Book of Mormon."

"Can you give supporting evidence for that position, Jim," Brother Moody prompted.

The boy leafed through his journal. "I only have one actual quote. A prominent non-Mormon, Doctor Fairchild, President of Oberlin College in Ohio, who had nothing to gain by his statement, wrote in a prominent newspaper in 1885—fifty-five years after the Book of Mormon was published: 'The theory of the origin of the Book of Mormon in the traditional manuscript of Solomon Spaulding will probably have to be relinquished.' He and other scholars had investigated the Spaulding manuscript in great detail and could detect no resemblance between the two."

"Can you tell us under what circumstances that statement was made?".

The boy glanced at Sal. "The Spaulding Manuscript had been lost since the early 1820's. President Fairchild found it in Hawaii in 1884." He closed his notebook quietly and looked down at his desk.

Sal felt like crawling under his desk. He was thankful for Brother Moody. "Is there any other evidence anyone would like to bring up?"

The rest of the day's class was a blur. He had prepared many arguments—arguments taken from the books he had read—but now none seemed to hold water. The longer he sat in class, the more upset he became. When Brother Moody dismissed the class he pushed through the other students and headed for the library. A touch on his elbow stopped him. It was the boy with glasses. Sal wished now he had taken time to learn his name— Brother Moody had called him Jim.

"I didn't mean to sound dogmatic," the youth said, almost apologetically, "but there is so much evidence against the Spaulding Manuscript that perhaps you will want to take some other challenges which are more realistic."

"Like what?" Sal said suspiciously.

"Oh, many issues have been raised against the Book of Mormon, like the location of the Hill Cumorah, or the apostasy of the witnesses."

Sal was still suspicious. Why would this person want to help him—especially after he was the one who had shot him down in class. "First," he said, "I'm going to look up your references and satisfy myself that what you said is true."

"Good."

Sal had calmed down by now. "What's your name?"

"Jim Moore."

By now they had arrived at the corner of the library. Amy had made no attempt to catch up with them, and Sal was not surprised. She had seemed embarrassed by his questions.

Jim stopped. "I have a science class now in the Eyring building," he said, "but I'd be glad to help where I can."

"You quoted a book in class. Can I get a copy of it?"

"Sure. It's a popular book among the Mormons. It's called the Articles of Faith and was written by Brother Talmage, an early apostle in the Church."

"Are there copies in the library?"

"I'm sure there are." Jim hesitated a moment and then said. "The library also has a copy of the Spaulding Manuscript. You can make the comparison yourself." Jim stuck out his hand. Sal, a little hesitantly, took it. After the handshake he watched Jim making his way through the mass of students on the sidewalk.

In the library he had no difficulty finding the Talmage book. There were dozens of them on the shelf. He leafed through it, noting it had been published a hundred years earlier. "Hah," he said to himself. "It's certainly not current." The book seemed to be a complete defense of the Mormon religion and its doctrines. Without having to refer to the Table of Contents, he found the chapter on the **Book of Mormon**. He skimmed the first part of the chapter. One point grabbed his attention. Talmage said, *"The final struggles between Nephites and Lamanites were waged in the vicinity of the Hill Cumorah, in what is now the State of New York, resulting in the destruction of the Nephites as a nation, about 400 A.D."*

"Eureka!" he said to himself thinking of what Jim had said as a possible challenge. "That's a serious discrepancy. Both the archaeology class and Brother Moody indicated Cumorah was in Central America." He carefully noted the reference, then continued reading.

He checked the book out of the library and took it home. He carefully read the author's remarks concerning the three witnesses: *though all of them withdrew from the Church and developed feelings amounting almost to hatred towards Joseph Smith, to the last of their lives they maintained the same solemn declaration of the angelic visit*. Jim had said he might use their story as a challenge.

He called Amy on the telephone. "Hi," he said brightly. "What do you know about the three witnesses?"

"Well," she said. "I know that even though they left the Church they never renounced their testimonies."

Sal nodded. To take that subject would be a trap. No, he would have to find something else.

Amy was still on the telephone. "Can I help you look up something?"

Sal was evasive. "No. I just heard about them and wanted to find more information." After visiting with her for a few minutes, he hung up.

So far, the only thing I can pursue is the Cumorah statement, he thought. He picked up the book and continued to read. Chapter fifteen was more of the same. It dealt with the authenticity of the book and cited several proofs. Hoping to find some discrepancy, Sal read and reread each

1. General agreement of the Book of Mormon with the Bible in all related matters. 2) Fulfillment of ancient prophecies accomplished by the bringing forth of the Book of Mormon. 3) Strict agreement and consistency of the Book of Mormon with itself. 4) Evident truth of its contained prophecies. 5) Corroborative testimony furnished by archaeology and ethnology.

Sal didn't even know what ethnology meant. He grabbed a dictionary from the shelf and looked it up: the study of a people's language. As he thoughtfully put the book back on the shelf he wondered aloud, "What does language have to do with the Book of Mormon" Nowhere did Talmage acknowledge the land bridge from Asia. Sal made a note of that. Didn't most scholars feel the Native Americans came that way from Asia?

He looked at the two questions he had written down. Not very much, but at least a start. Perhaps he would have to use sources outside of the book to prove it false.

He completed the chapter and still hadn't found the quotation concerning the Spaulding manuscript. He glanced at his watch. He was late for class.

Amy seemed a little stand-offish. "What's the matter?" he asked.

She shook her head. "I'm just not sure that what you are doing is going to help you understand and gain a testimony of the Book of Mormon." They walked to the Wilkinson Center.

"I am really learning a lot," Sal said lamely.

"Yes, but is it what you should be learning?" She changed the subject abruptly. "How's your tennis coming?"

"I think I made the traveling team," he said. "What are we eating tonight?"

"You go ahead and eat," she said. "I'll eat dinner with the family tonight."

He grabbed a salad, several hard-shell tacos, and a caffeine-free Diet Pepsi. After paying for the meal they found a small booth. "Don't you want anything?" Sal asked.

"No," she said, shaking her head.

Feeling a little miserable, he started eating. He wanted nothing more than to please Amy, yet always seemed to fail at that task.

"Sal," Amy said, "You know how much I care for you?"

"Mm-hmm," he grunted, not looking up, his mouth full of taco.

"Then, why can't you study the Book of Mormon like everyone else?"

He finished chewing, using the time to formulate his thoughts. "Amy, the primary reason I'm in the class at all is to be with you. I'm trying to do what you want me to—find out if the Book of Mormon is true. I just have to do it my own way, I guess," he finished lamely. He finally looked at Amy. Her eyes were moist, the beginnings of tears about to erupt.

That night in the apartment, he reread the notes he had prepared on the Spaulding Manuscript. There must have been a hundred. He was about to throw all of them in the trash when the telephone rang.

"Hi," he said.

"Hi, Sal," the voice on the other end was faint and Sal had to listen closely to even hear. "This is Jim Moore."

"How did you find my phone number?" "It's easy with the campus directory. Sal, I hope you don't mind my calling, but I have some information for you. Do you mind if I come over for a minute?"

Sal thought of all the studying he needed to do this evening. "No," he said, "come on over. I had some questions to ask you, anyway."

"Great," Jim said. "I'll be there about 7:30."

Before Jim hardly had a chance to step inside, Sal asked him, "Why are you doing this?"

Jim smiled shyly. "I've been an underdog all my life, and I hate to see anyone take a licking."

"That isn't the impression I got this afternoon," Sal said sourly.

"Oh, that," Jim said. "If I hadn't raised the point someone else would have. I'm afraid when it comes to challenging the Book of Mormon you are all by yourself in that class—even if Brother Moody is trying to help you."

Sal nodded. "Have a seat?"

Jim sat down and pulled out his briefcase.

"Before you do that," Sal said. "What about all of these quotes about the Spaulding Manuscript. There must be a hundred of them."

"How many of the people making the statements have read either the Spaulding Manuscript or the Book of Mormon" Jim asked quietly.

"I don't know," Sal said sarcastically. "Most of the statements were made during the 1800's."

"Let me see them," Jim said. He riffled through them, one after another. "What did you notice that was similar in every one of them," he asked.

Sal reread the quotes over Jim's shoulder. He had found some similarity. "All of them quote from a book called *Mormonism Unveiled*," he said.

"That is where every one of these people got their information. None of them could actually read the Spaulding Manuscript—it was lost until 1884." Jim put the papers down. "It's a case of everyone grasping at a single straw to justify their opposition to the Book of Mormon So all of these so-called scholars just quoted the same piece of unverified information."

Sal took the papers, wadded them up, and threw them in the wastebasket. "Which reminds me. I never did find the quote about the president of whats-it college in this book." He slammed the Talmage book down on the table.

"Oh. Dr. Fairchild, President of Oberlin College." Jim took the book and thumbed through it. "It's been my experience when reading Talmage, you will find the most information in the footnotes rather the text. Here."

Sal made a mental note. Page 502 in the chapter notes. Jim read it aloud once more and looked up. "That seems clear enough," Sal said. "Now my concern is, where do I go from here?"

"I don't know if you want to pursue it," Jim said, "but just like the Spaulding Manuscript has been the most obnoxious thorn to Book of Mormon scholars, within the Church one of the most persistent apparent inconsistencies deals with the location of the Hill Cumorah."

Sal didn't tell Jim he had already found that discrepancy.

Jim said, "Many General Authorities persist in their approach that the Hill Cumorah is in upstate New York. But all of the archaeological evidence points to a location in Central America." He looked at Sal. "Maybe that will give you something to study and challenge the class with."

Sal was still suspicious of Jim's motives. "So where do I go from here?"

Jim shrugged. "That's something you'll have to work out. Just remember, archaeology is not a strong suit of most of the students in our class. Maybe you can pull something off." He looked at his watch. "Well, gotta go. Good luck, Sal."

After Jim left, Sal stood at the door and watched his small, retreating back. "I wonder what axe he has to grind?" he said to himself.

The next day he searched for material concerning Cumorah. His first break came when he pulled down Mormondom's own reference encyclopedia, Mormon Doctrine, by McConkie. He wrote the quote on a 3 x 5 card: *Both the Nephite and Jaredite civilizations fought their final great wars of extinction at and near the Hill Cumorah, which hill is located between Palmyra and Manchester in the western part of the state of New York.* A footnote at the bottom of McConkie's statement led him to Joseph Fielding Smith's book, Gospel Doctrine III.

What a goldmine! Smith, who had been a prominent apostle and even president of the Mormon Church took an adamant view on the subject. Smith even quoted from the Prophet Joseph Smith, Oliver Cowdery, David Whitmer and others. Sal carefully wrote down all the references on cards. He'd show the class. He took notes with him from Orson Pratt, Joseph Smith, Oliver Cowdery, Bruce R. McConkie, and Joseph Fielding Smith supporting the New York Cumorah, He felt pretty secure in his position. He also carried a stack of scholarly books to class which favored a location for Cumorah somewhere in Central America.

Greeting Brother Moody with a smile, he took the desk chair next to Amy and squeezed her hand. He listened quietly during the first part of the class, then, when ready, turned and winked at Jim. Jim smiled back. "Brother Moody," he said. "In my archaeology class the professor has repeatedly said the Hill Cumorah as spoken of in the Book of Mormon is located in Central America. I have a stack of texts here which all support that theory with archaeological and"—he looked at his notes—"ethnological evidence. You have also alluded to that. Yet, in my reading concerning such an important thing, every Mormon Church leader consistently placed Cumorah in upstate New York. Can you explain this discrepancy?"

There was a short period of silence. No hands went up in the class—not even the smart-alecky girl in the front row. Brother Moody finally responded. "Sal, as you have noted, there is a great difference concerning belief about that particular point." He spread his arms to the class. "Do any of you care to explain why this is?"

Again, there were no hands raised. Sal waited an appropriate amount of time, and asked if he could recite from his notes. He gave the Talmage quote, the McConkie quote, quoted extensively from Joseph Fielding Smith, paraphrased the words of Orson Pratt concerning Cumorah, and wound up by talking about the incident during the Zion's March when Joseph Smith identified a skeleton as a white Lamanite who had died in that area—the area of Cumorah.

Rod, the returned missionary, raised his hand. "Since we follow a living prophet, if the prophets say Cumorah is in upstate New York, then Cumorah must be in upstate New York."

That was what Sal had been waiting for. He raised his hand again and pointed to the big stack of books on his desk. "There is almost unanimous opinion by the people who wrote these books— mostly scholars from BYU—that Cumorah is in Central America. Who is right? Where is the real Cumorah?"

Sal was facing the front so he didn't see Jim Moore's hand tentatively raise, but Brother Moody did. "Jim?"

Sal turned in his desk and looked at Jim, who had helped him. Would he shoot him down, now?

"I have no answer for Sal," Jim said quietly. "Church leaders are not infallible, though." He shuffled through his papers. "Sal quoted President Joseph Fielding Smith, concerning Cumorah. President Smith also said," he held his notes close to his huge glasses, "'You cannot accept the books written by the authorities of the Church as standards of doctrine, only in so far as they accord with the revealed word and the standard works. Every man who writes is responsible, not the Church, for what he writes.'"

There was no further discussion. Sal glowed inside. Brother Moody seemed impressed. Class was over. Students left quietly, hardly discussing.

Brother Moody called, "Sal, may I see you a moment."

Sal squeezed Amy's hand. "I'll catch up with you."

"Never mind," she said. "I'll wait for you." "Sal, that was excellent research," Brother Moody said. "If you will write up your findings, both pro and con, that will constitute your final exam."

"Thank you," Sal beamed. "Brother Moody, I must admit there were few discrepancies I could find concerning the Book of Mormon."

Brother Moody looked at Sal. "There really isn't a controversy with this point, either, Sal. The General Authorities of the Church have just never worried about geography or other evidences."

Sal opened his mouth to speak, but Brother Moody kept talking.

"But you need to know that those same General Authorities are the ones who sit as a Board of Trustees for this university. They are the ones who encouraged the archaeology, anthropology, and geography departments to develop their theories concerning Book of Mormon geography."

"Why didn't you say that in class?"

"Frankly, I wanted the impact of what you said to hit the class and give them something to think about,"

Brother Moody said. "Besides, it is a valid point and needs further study."

CHAPTER 4

Amy wiped tears from her eyes as they walked from class. With her free hand she clasped her books tightly to her breast.

"What's wrong?" Sal asked, concern in his voice.

"I can't understand how you can question what I believe in so strongly." There was a tremor in her voice as she continued. "Maybe my brothers are right. Maybe I shouldn't be getting so serious with you." Tears broke free and rolled down her cheeks. "All you do is criticize. You act as if you don't want to learn about the Church."

Sal gritted his teeth in his frustration. "Amy, I thought you understood. I have to learn about the Church in my own way." He spread his hands in his anxiety. "Besides, your brothers don't like me because I'm Hispanic."

"Your own way? What way is that? All you ever do is question everything, trying to undermine Brother Moody's teachings."

"Brother Moody gave me the opportunity to investigate the Book of Mormon according to logic and the evidence. That's what I'm doing. I'm not trying to undermine his or anyone else's teachings."

Sal could see that Amy was still not satisfied. He took her hand. "Please understand," he pleaded. "Everything I do is only to please you. You are more important to me than anything."

She squeezed his hands, but without saying anything.

The final exam schedule was posted and Sal dutifully attended each exam session.

Amy seemed as anxious as he that he get good grades. "How did you do?" she asked.

"I figure I've earned at least a 3.5 GPA. I think I'll get an 'A' out of Brother Moody. Tennis is an automatic 'A' and I'll split some "A"s and "B"s in my other classes. The only class I'm worried about is archaeology. It has turned out very heavy, with lots of reading and research. The final was also a humdinger."

They stopped at the Cougar Bar for lunch. Over a strawberry milkshake Amy asked, "Are you going to attend Summer Semester?"

"I don't know. I need to earn money for next year."

"What about your scholarship and job?"

"The tennis scholarship only covers books and tuition, and my job in the receiving department has been the pits." He sipped his drink and then laughed. "In the short time I've been at the "Y" I've unloaded tons of toilet paper, copy paper, toner, ink, and paper towels."

"But it has kept you in school."

"Yes. It's given me enough money to pay my apartment rent and a little food, but," he laughed self-consciously, "there's never enough left over for dates."

They finished lunch and headed back into the Eyring Center to see if grades had been posted. A large poster caught Sal's eye.

He looked closer for details. A selected group of students would tour Book of Mormon lands, ending at the proposed site of the Mesoamerica Cumorah in Southern Mexico. Those archaeology students chosen to participate in the dig would have the tour and their board and room paid for.

"Amy, look at this," he exclaimed. "If I can get on the dig I can experience first hand what I've been writing about."

Amy was less than enthusiastic. She pouted, "I don't want you gone all summer."

"The dig will also furnish the field experience in archaeology I've been wanting," he said, his excitement showing in his voice. "What an opportunity! This is the chance I've been waiting for."

"What do you mean," she said suspiciously.

"Can't you see," he replied. "This gives me a chance to verify the Book of Mormon by hard scientific evidence."

She shook her head. "I still can't understand why you can't get a testimony like everyone else. Why do you have to do these crazy things?"

Sal was disappointed. An inspiration hit him. "Would you at least come with me to talk to Brother Moody about it?"

Neither of them said a word until they sat in Brother Moody's office in the Joseph Smith building. Sal spoke first. "Brother Moody, we appreciate your taking time to talk to us."

Brother Moody smiled.

Sal looked earnestly at Amy as he spoke. "Brother Moody, I truly want to get a testimony of the Book of Mormon"

Amy interrupted him. "But he insists on doing it his own way."

"Amy gets upset at me when I challenge anything concerning the Book of Mormon I just want to be scientific and logical." He looked at Brother Moody, who just nodded, so Sal continued. "An archaeology tour of Mexico and Central America is scheduled for this summer, with a dig at the site of the proposed Cumorah. With the research I've done so far, I'd like to participate on this dig and hopefully learn the truth about the Book of Mormon" He wiped sweat from his forehead.

"So, what prevents you?"

"I guess I'm the culprit," Amy spoke up. "To me, it is more important for Sal to just read the Book of Mormon and pray about it and stay here this summer."

Smiling, Brother Moody leaned back in his chair, his hands clasped behind his head. Long—or so it seemed to Sal—moments passed before he spoke. "Let me propose something to both of you," he said. "You didn't know this, but I will be one of the tour directors. Amy, why don't you take the tour with us? We can discuss the Book of Mormon lands together as we tour. Sal can do his research and you and I can get a deeper understanding of the Book of Mormon"

Sal's eyes were shining. *Amy with me!*

"Mom and Dad could afford to send me," she said tentatively. She looked again at Brother Moody. "Do you really feel this can help Sal get a testimony?"

Brother Moody leaned forward and looked intensely at her. "Amy, I have directed over twenty tours to the Book of Mormon lands. Each time, my own testimony is strengthened. The Church has never really explored the logical side of testimony. If Sal goes on the tour with us, he will probably come away with a testimony." He picked up a pencil from his desk and played with it. "Amy, many people have had to get a testimony of something first by living and experiencing it before they were ever able to get a witness of the Spirit. Sal's idea is a good one. I can even put in a good word with the archaeology department—after all, Sal has already given us a lot to think about Cumorah—so they will approve him for the dig scholarship."

Beaming, Sal looked at Amy. Impulsively, she turned and smiled at him, opened her mouth and laughed. "It seems to me that we are going to be spending time together in Mexico."

"Not only Mexico, but also Guatemala," Brother Moody smiled.

"I wonder if Jim Moore can go, too," Sal said impulsively.

Within the week Sal's name was listed as a scholarship recipients. Sal was disappointed that Jim hadn't even applied. Amy had no difficulty talking her parents into covering the cost of the tour. Their only concern was proper supervision. Brother Moody was able to handle that question. Now, they were all set.

At the BYU Travel Study department where they paid Amy's fee, the receptionist handed each of them a thick, blue looseleaf binder. "You will need to study these materials prior to the tour," she said. "There are also several things you must complete and return to this office before you leave. Please return the green waiver and release form and the pink beneficiary form."

"Beneficiary form?" Amy asked.

"Included in your fee is a life insurance policy." Seeing Amy's wide eyes, the woman quickly added. "Not that we think anything is going to happen, but we do like to be prepared." She looked down at her checklist of instructions. Sal listened carefully as she talked of immunization records and other requirements. He didn't want to screw up.

"Do you have passports?" the woman asked.

"I hadn't even thought of getting a passport."

The woman glanced at the calendar. "It will take a minimum of two weeks to get a passport."

"Where do we apply?"

"There's a new postal passport service. I have the forms and address right here."

Sal wondered if everyone had to go through all of the same kind of hassle. But finally, they were finished. "That was a nightmare."

"She was really trying to be helpful," Amy said. "But it does tire me." She pointed to a bench. "Let's go through the manual."

"Wow, they think of everything," Sal said, as he looked at the index. "Even songs to sing while we travel through the romantic countryside. Maybe there are some love songs," he teased. The general information section gave information on immunizations, insurance, a trip-planning checklist, packing tips, advice for international travelers, and even information from the U.S. Customs Office.

The second section on Country Information was more interesting. It included BYU Culturegrams for Mexico and Guatemala, a list of study aids, a map of their tour, a suggested reading list, and thumbnail sketches of some of the cities and ruins they would be visiting.

The third section was the itinerary. "This shows us flying from Salt Lake City to Mexico City on June 18." "That's a Thursday," Sal said glancing at his watch. "It's only three weeks away." He waited until Amy read through the days' planning, then closed the book. He stared at Mount Timpanogas, a slight frown on his handsome, Hispanic face.

"What are you thinking about?" Amy prodded.

He turned and smiled at her. "Two things," he said. "One, all we have to get done before we go."

"And?"

"That I am going to have you all to myself for two whole weeks." He leaned over and pecked her on the nose.

Three weeks passed rapidly, what with getting paperwork done, clearing up things in the apartment, selecting the items to take, getting passports, shots, and everything else. Sal even boned up on his Spanish. He had not spoken a word of Spanish since leaving his home the previous fall—and then only because that was his mother's chosen language.

The bus picked them up at the BYU parking lot at 5:30 A.M. Sal grumbled. "People have to be mad"—he looked at Amy—"or in love, to get up this early." He loaded their suitcases on the bus. Once on the bus, he and Amy held hands all the way to the Salt Lake City airport. Sal didn't know they were holding hands, though. He was sound asleep as soon as the bus started from the parking lot.

The airport, even at that early hour, resembled a beehive. People scurried here and there. Lines seemed to go on forever at the ticket counters. The travel representative met them at the entry, had them stack their luggage in a heap by the ticket counter, and directed them to the "D" concourse where the Delta direct flight to Mexico City waited.

This was the first opportunity Sal and Amy had of seeing all who were on the tour. Brother Moody waved at them—the only other person they knew out of the group of fourteen people. Sal did recognize Dr. Bingham from the archaeology department. He walked to where Brother Moody stood. "Is this the whole group?" he asked.

Brother Moody smiled. "No. Others will join us in Mexico City." He looked at his list. "There will be forty-two all together."

A short wait at the gate, and soon they boarded the airplane. Sal had never flown before. Everything seemed new and interesting. He let Amy have the window seat. As they buckled their seat belts, he leaned over and whispered, "Amy, the most exciting thing about this whole trip is that we are doing it together."

The airplane shuddered as it started down the runway. As the engines thrummed to full power, Sal gripped the seat arms tightly, the back of his head pressed into the seat. He jerked as the pilot pulled the plane off the ground and the wheels thumped into their wells. Once they were airborne, he finally could look out the windows. He watched as they climbed above the Salt Lake valley and through the mountains. Once they reached altitude, they were so high Sal couldn't make out any terrain features. The flight actually became boring. He finally rested his head on Amy's shoulder and slept. Amy awakened him for lunch. He enjoyed the sandwich and salad.

"Do you think we ought to study?" she asked.

Sal exaggerated a stretch. "Since we will be getting credit for the tour, perhaps we could crack the books."

One of the books recommended was David Palmer's In Search of Cumorah. Amy picked up a copy of it at the bookstore just before the tour. She opened it now and held it between them. The first chapter was titled: "Why Search for Cumorah?" Sal sat up a little straighter. The chapter started with a quote from Joseph Smith: *It would not be a bad plan to compare Mr. Stephen's ruined cities with those in the Book of Mormon. Light cleaves to light and facts are supported by facts. The truth injures no one...*

"Who is this Mr. Stephens?"

"I don't know," Amy replied. "We'll have to ask Brother Moody."

They read on silently through the chapter, commenting now and again as they read something that piqued their mutual curiosity. When they finished, Sal sighed. "That answers every question I raised in class about the two Cumorahs. Brother Moody could have put me down right then."

"But he didn't."

"No," Sal said. "I guess he really did want us to do some thinking on our own."

Sal felt the plane starting to nose down. He glanced past Amy out of the window. All he could see were clouds beneath them. The captain's voice rasped through the intercom. "Ladies and gentlemen, we are beginning our initial descent into the Valley of Mexico. After we break through the clouds we will fly low over the city on our approach path. This is an unusual day in Mexico—there is little smog. Take advantage of it while you can."

The voice of the flight attendant broke in. "Please adjust your seats to the full upright position..."

Sal listened with half an ear as he gazed past Amy out the window, waiting for his first view of the city.

The landing was smooth and soon they were in a line leading to passport check and customs. It seemed so mechanical, Sal thought. The officials seemed almost uninterested or bored with their work. When he had picked up his and Amy's bags and loaded them on a cart, they wheeled out to the customs inspector. He motioned Sal to push a button. When he did a green light flashed on the pillar and the agent waved them through.

"You mean that's all there is to customs?" he asked incredulously. "I thought they would go through every bag."

"That's it," Brother Moody said as he came up behind them. He smiled. "If you get the red light, they search your luggage with a fine-tooth comb." He walked ahead and motioned them to follow him.

Other people waited at the bus parking area. People introduced themselves and the total group clambered aboard the bus. Everybody seemed excited; the noise level high. Brother Moody picked up the microphone and held his hand up for silence. Slowly conversations died down until he could be heard. "Brothers and sisters," he began. "We welcome you to the Lands of the Book of Mormon Tour. This will be one of the highlights of your life—one you will hold sacred. I would recommend that you keep a journal of your thoughts and experiences. We will have a tour orientation tomorrow morning at the hotel. Our time is extremely limited so that's all I am going to say today. Get a good night's sleep tonight." A few seconds later the loud speaker buzzed again. Brother Moody added, "One other thing. Your luggage has either a red or a green tag. Those with red tags will be staying at the Hotel Holiday Inn Crowne Plaza. The bus will stop there first. Those with green tags are members of the archaeological group who will remain in Mexico following the tour. Arrangements have been made to house you in private homes in the Mexico City area."

Sal moaned. "That means we will be separated." Squeezing his hand, Amy said. "It's okay, silly. We are only going to be here for a few days— and we will be spending the days and evenings together."

Chapter 5

The air-conditioned bus dropped Amy and the regular tour group off at the hotel. Sal slumped in his seat. Soon the excitement of being in Mexico City pulled him erect. He gawked at the buildings and read the street signs as the bus looped around the city on the Circuito Interior highway. Traffic filled the highway in endless lines. Hundreds of yellow and black Volkswagen bug taxis darted in and out of traffic. The bus entered a huge park—Chapultepec—and finally turned onto a broad boulevard, Paseo de La Reforma. Houses along Reforma caught his attention: fantastic, huge colonial-style mansions, lots of wrought iron, white stucco, stone, tiers of windows, gabled roofs, turrets, high fences. The bus made a turn and stopped. A large stone fence blocked any view of the house inside.

Dr. Bingham, the dig director, announced, "Here is where we will stay. Our host is Leon Hamilton. He is a bank director and is bishop of a Spanish-speaking ward. He and his gracious wife, RaNae, have opened their home to you for the next few days. Please treat this as a rare privilege."

Sal stepped off the bus. The driver unloaded the baggage and piled it by the imposing, locked door. Dr. Bingham stepped into a side niche and pressed a button. "Bueno?" a woman's sound-amplified voice came through the speaker above his head. In fluent Spanish Dr. Bingham announced who they were. Immediately the big double door split in the middle and swung open.

Sal picked up his bag and walked inside. Wow! he thought. He had never seen such a home. Colonnades held up a portico above the driveway. The sparkling, white, four-story house seemed to have every light on. Students, in apparent awe, crowded closer together. Dr. Bingham led the way. The door under the portico opened. A tall, handsome Anglo man greeted them.

"Students," Dr. Bingham said, "this is Bishop Hamilton." He extended his hand. "Bishop, again, we thank you for the privilege of using your home." The Bishop's voice was pleasant and well-modulated. "As I told you before, Earl, we enjoy having you here." He laughed. "Besides, how else can I satisfy my own amateur archaeology interests."

Dr. Bingham turned and introduced each of the students. Bishop Hamilton shook their hands and greeted them warmly. Sal was impressed with the firmness of the man's grip and his direct eye contact. That's something I still lack, he thought. Dr. Bingham continued, "Bishop Hamilton has participated on a number of digs, including some of the very earliest work with Dr. Palmer on the Hill Vigia, site of our proposed Central America Cumorah."

Sal was suitably impressed. "Just put your luggage by the door," the bishop interposed. "Sebastian will take care of it. Then come in and meet my wife." He chuckled. "She's more of an archaeologist than I am."

The entry way, done in warm walnut, featured a shiny, white tile floor. The marble continued through the living room but an oriental-type rug covered it. They pushed into the kitchen, which was huge—bigger than Sal's mother's whole apartment.

Sister Hamilton—RaNae, as she asked to be called—was a perfect hostess. She was in the kitchen with the maid, whom she introduced as Guadalupe, preparing small sandwiches and Mexican finger foods. She insisted they all sit around the huge family table and eat.

Sal felt an immediate kinship to Guadalupe. He went up to her and spoke in Spanish, "Senora Guadalupe, my mother's name is also Guadalupe."

She beamed and rattled off something in Spanish so fast that even Sal had a hard time getting all of it. Something about how glad she was that he was here and how well he spoke Spanish, and she would like to meet his mother.

None of the other students had spoken. They still seemed cowed by the immensity and grandeur of the home. Brother Bingham asked RaNae, "Where are your children?"

"Mary's in California attending a cousin's wedding. Robert is off on some youth activity with his ward, and I let Tammy and Sue go to a movie with some friends." She deftly set a plate of steaming tortillas in front of the students, followed by plates of cheeses, meats, jams, peppers and sauces. She smiled warmly at the students, "If any of you get hungry during the night, there are plenty of things in the refrigerator. There is even a microwave in which you can heat anything."

"What about the water?" a student asked.

"Bottled water and several kinds of juices are in the fridge," she said. "I wouldn't advise you to drink the water out of the taps." She laughed merrily. "It does funny things to people."

"That will be the rule on the entire trip," interposed Dr. Bingham. "Drink only bottled water and juices."

After their snack the bishop took them on a tour of his house. Sal was impressed. White marble floors, a huge curving staircase leading from the living room to the second floor, a small den off the living room that looked like a museum with all kinds of pottery and statuary. Every room held books and study materials. Upstairs was a TV room and library, off which were the bishop's office and half a dozen bedrooms. One of the bedrooms was obviously a small girls' room. The bed was heaped with dolls—

more dolls than Sal had seen in any store. A huge walk-in closet led to a large bathroom with double sinks and a marble shower.

Bishop Hamilton stopped, his foot on the stair that led up to the fourth floor. "There is room for all of you upstairs. Sebastian will have already taken your bags up. You know where the shower is. Feel free to shower or hit the sack now, or you can join Dr. Bingham and me for a short discussion on archaeology."

Sal elected for the discussion. Bishop Hamilton and Dr. Bingham made themselves comfortable on the couch in the downstairs den. The students sat around on the floor, surrounded by specimens of pottery and statuary—all with an ancient look. "Let me introduce some of these pieces," the bishop said. He explained artifacts he had bought and those he had dug himself. Several axelike pieces of obsidian had come from the Hill Vigia—where they would soon be digging themselves. "Earl," he asked the professor. "Are you any closer now to making some definite claims about Cumorah?"

"Possibly more dealing with language than with artifacts."

"Language? What do you mean?"

"Leon, you are aware that many of Mexico's mountains, lakes, rivers and cities carry Nahuatl or Aztec names. One of the hills near Vigia is Cintepec, which in Nahuatl means 'corn hill.'" He turned to his students. "In Nahuatl, 'tepec' means hill or mountain, of which there are many examples. 'Cin' means corn, thus Cintepec—'corn hill.'

"Cintepec is fairly close to the Hill Vigia, which we feel is the leading candidate for the location where the last great battles of the Book of Mormon were fought. You will remember also, that Shim is the name of a hill in the Book of Mormon where Ammaron told Mormon he would find the records. Mormon went there when he was twenty-four. The interesting thing is, 'Shim' in the Maya language also means corn. Therefore, Cintepec, the hill that is close to the Hill Vigia, possibly could be the Hill Shim mentioned in the Book of Mormon. It might be of interest that the huge Olmec stone heads discovered along the Gulf of Mexico were carved from stone quarried from Cintepec, and since the Olmec culture dates to the Jaredite culture ..." he left the sentence dangling.

Wow, Sal thought to himself. Bishop Hamilton nodded. "That all makes good sense." He pulled a large, illustrated book from a stack on the table before him. "Earl, have you had a chance to read this?" Sal looked at the title, *The Blood of Kings, Dynasty and Ritual in Maya Art.*

Dr. Bingham shook his head.

Brother Hamilton continued. "The are work in it is beautiful, but dealing with archaeology, the the most important contribution of the book is in its presentation and interpretation of glyphs." He opened the book and showed pages filled with panels of black and white drawings—glyphs. He laughed. "In fact, on this page is one that all Mormons should appreciate." He showed it to Dr. Bingham, who chuckled.

"And it came to pass. Perhaps that explains why Joseph Smith, in translating the Book of Mormon, used that phrase so much."

"And it came to pass is a real stumbling block for many of those reading the Book of Mormon for the first time," Bishop Hamilton said, "but, since we have found glyphs with that meaning it should actually strengthen the testimonies of those who read the Book of Mormon."

Sal nodded his head.

Bishop Hamilton stood up. "I would like to stay up and visit longer, Earl, but I have a board of director's meeting first thing in the morning. Perhaps we can continue our discussion tomorrow evening."

Sleep wouldn't come to Sal. He didn't know why he felt so excited. Here he lay in the land of his ancestors, finding out about a book he had rejected. Through this trip, he thought as he lay there, I will find the answers to my questions.

Guadalupe served them breakfast before the bus picked them up. Sal watched as they drove through the city. He had never seen so many automobiles in his life. Most streets were three lanes wide with bumper-to-bumper traffic.

Dr. Bingham cut into his thoughts. "What do you think about the world's biggest city?"

"Looks like the world's biggest traffic jam," Sal said flippantly as he looked out the window.

"With little relief in sight," the professor added.

At the hotel Brother Moody had already begun his orientation. He motioned the students to take seats and continued. "As I indicated, today will be a tour of what are probably the most famous ruins in Mexico—Teotihuacan. The well-preserved pyramids are about 45 minutes northeast of Mexico City. According to our carbon-dating, Teotihuacan was probably occupied from about 150 B.C. to 750 A.D. Tradition reports that Teotihuacan was a religious center. The ancient Teotihuacan culture was referred to by the later Aztec culture as 'the place of the gods' or 'the place where men became gods.' As far as our study is concerned, the founding of Teotihuacan seems to parallel the 50 BC migration of those Book of Mormon people who left the land of Zarahemla and went to the Land Northward. If Teotihuacan is the Land Northward, then the city played a major role in the final downfall of the Nephite nation. Be aware that archaeologically, Teotihuacan is a non-Book of Mormon or Mayan culture.

"The Valley of Mexico, where you are presently located, has been homeland of many civilizations, including the Aztecs who arrived here in about 1325 AD. Nephite immigrants probably moved into the Valley of Mexico about 50 BC and played a significant role in Nephite history from that time to about 400 AD. Now, let's board the bus and start our drive. We'll talk as we go."

On the bus, Brother Moody said, "Sometimes Teotihuacan is simply referred to as 'the pyramids.' The two main pyramids, Pyramid of the Sun, and Pyramid of the Moon, are the most imposing structures."

Amy scribbled madly to take notes on everything Brother Moody said.

"I want you to pay special attention to the Temple of Quetzalcoatl. I think you will find the Christian theme very apparent in its structure."

Sal and Amy hung close to Brother Moody during the tour of Teotihuacan. There was so much to see, but so much needed interpretation. They tried to ignore the hundreds of children, men, and women, selling curios and trinkets. Curios, laid out on multi-colored Indian blankets, even covered the top of the Temple of the Sun.

"During the period of 150 BC to 200 AD," Brother Moody said as they stood on the top of the spectacular pyramid, "the city expanded to occupy more than twelve square miles. The people fell into various social classes, represented by artisans, farmers, architects, painters, sculptors, businessmen, priests, and government officials."

"What did the farmers raise for food?" Amy asked.

"About the same as today," Brother Moody responded. "Archaeologists have found remains of beans, corn, squash, and other fruits and vegetables. Another plant which is still harvested today is the maguey plant."

"What was it used for?" one of the women asked.

"A variety of uses, from medicine to food. But the most popular use of maguey is the extraction of a juice called pulque, which is fermented to make a popular liquor."

As they started down the steep steps, Brother Moody continued. "Notice the use of cement. One of the earliest criticisms of the Book of Mormon was that it mentioned the use of cement in construction. Like every other criticism of the Book of Mormon, that has long ago been debunked. The reasons are all around you."

Sal studied the construction of the pyramids and other buildings: Lava rocks held in place with cement; floors also of cement. Plaster covered most of the buildings and some buildings, he could tell, had murals and frescoes painted in brilliant colors.

"These murals are from what we call Teotihuacan Period II," Brother Moody said. "That was the period from about 200 AD to 350 AD. In that period the people began their worship of a veritable pantheon of gods, foremost of which was the feathered-serpent god called Quetzalcoatl."

As they climbed the Temple of the Moon—far down the Avenue of the Dead—Brother Moody continued with his explanation. "The square of the Temple of the Moon was completed during what we call Teotihuacan Period III—between 350 AD and 600 AD. During this time the population of the city reached almost 200,000 inhabitants. It was by far the largest city in this hemisphere, and probably the largest city in the world at that time."

Little was said as they walked to the Temple of Quetzalcoatl. Everyone seemed in awe. Finally, Amy asked quietly, "Why did they abandon the city? Why did it die?"

Brother Moody didn't answer for a moment. Then he said, "No one, of course is sure why Teotihuacan died. One archaeologist surmised that the principal reason for the decline of Teotihuacan was the excessive power of the priests, military and merchants. Their abuse of that power caused people to rebel and society broke up."

At the Temple Of Quetzalcoatl. Brother Moody pointed out the symbolism of twelve, and the godhead symbols, which seemed to predominate.

"Why Quetzalcoatl?" one of the tour members asked.

"I think the title of Quetzalcoatl came about as a result of the visit of the resurrected Christ to the

Nephites," Brother Moody responded. "From various accounts handed down, Quetzalcoatl was born of a virgin, came from the East, dressed in a long white robe, taught the people the law of the fast, instructed them in baptism, died, and three days later was resurrected. When he left he prophesied his people would pass through much persecution but he would return and they would in turn become lords of the earth."

It was almost too much for Sal to digest. Here he was seeing the monuments, the symbolism, and now it appeared most of it came from Jesus Christ. "Boy, am I confused," he muttered.

"What?" Amy asked.

"Nothing," he said. "I'm just getting hungry."

Following a sack lunch on the bus, they rode back to the city. In the center of Chapultepec Park a magnificent building reared above them. Spanish words across the front, which Sal translated for Amy, proclaimed, NATIONAL MUSEUM OF ANTHROPOLOGY.

Sal smiled as he looked around the parking lot. Several youngsters, clothed in bright colors, practiced bull-fighting. One, dressed in the regalia of a bullfighter, deftly avoided the charge of a child pushing a set of widespread horns mounted on wheels. Others sitting on the curb, acted as the cheering section for those in the "arena."

Hundreds of people, hawkers and gawkers, filled the plaza before the museum. Peddlers sold pottery, jade and dozens of other items. Others people sat on the terraces, visiting, thinking, or staring.

"Here, you are on your own," Brother Moody advised. "English-speaking tours begin every fifteen minutes. I would recommend you stick with a tour and hear what the natives have to say about their history and culture."

"Where will you be?" Amy asked him.

"I think I will just wander around and see some of my favorite displays."

"Would you mind terribly if we just stayed with you?" Amy asked.

He smiled indulgently. "You're welcome."

The entrance led to a large enclosed patio area. Dominating the patio was a huge architectural wonder—what looked like an gigantic upside-down umbrella with water cascading over its edges into a reflection pool. Hundreds of people sat around the patio area, reading, reflecting, resting. Room, after room, after room, filled with archaeological and anthropological wonders—Olmec, Maya, Aztec, Teotihuacan, and seemingly dozens of other cultures—fascinated Sal.

He could understand why people sat on benches on the patio. It was almost too much. His head swam with it all. What a heritage Mexico had! By that same token, he thought, what a heritage I have! In the entrance to the Teotihuacan Room was a wall plaque. Sal translated it to Amy:

Before there was light
Before there was day
When it was still dark
The gods met in council
In Teotihuacan.

"I wish they used English to explain these things," Amy pouted. "Everything is written in Spanish."

"I'll interpret," Sal laughed. "I think I finally understand what Brother Moody said about the priests of Teotihuacan," he said.

Amy looked at him quizzically.

"According to these exhibits the priestly class, at the pinnacle of Teotihuacan society, lived in sumptuous mansions beside the temples. The priests," he continued, "not the common people, became experts in writing, in the calendar, in mathematics, and astronomy. They governed every aspect of life, from reading the stars to directing the peasants when to plant their crops."

Amy was wide-eyed, taking it all in.

"The exhibits show dramatically how big the business of institutionalized religion became," Brother Moody said. "The gods, images, temples and priests proliferated. Religion became the main drawing card of the city."

"I am still not sure how all of this ties into the Book of Mormon" Sal said, turning to him.

Brother Moody looked thoughtfully at the model of the city before him. "No one knows for sure. Teotihuacan could have been settled by people other than those in the Book of Mormon But there are several possible ways they could be tied in. Teotihuacan might have been settled by the people who were considered 'robbers' by the Nephites. Therefore the people of Teotihuacan would be unfriendly or even antagonistic to the Nephites."

"And?"

"Another possibility is that because it was a religious center, Teotihuacan was passive during the final battle. Because the dates link, my personal hunch is the elite of Teotihuacan were actually Nephites. They were exterminated at Cumorah, which accounts for the abandonment of the Avenue of the Dead at the time of the last Nephite battle."

"So Teotihuacan was a Nephite City?" Amy asked.

"Not necessarily," Brother Moody replied. "The influence of Teotihuacan actually increased after the destruction of the Nephites in 385 AD."

It was late afternoon by the time they completed their tour of the museum. Their last stop had been a marvelous exhibit on the Mayas.

"What was most exciting for you?" Sal asked as they walked from the building back to the patio.

"I liked the Aztec exhibit—the one with the huge calendar stone." Amy looked at him. "I am so filled with information, though, it is hard to say. The main reason I like the calendar stone is because it is the thing I have read most about. What about you?"

Sal looked up at the huge umbrella-like water display. "I guess I still liked the Teotihuacan exhibition room best, even thought Brother Moody did show me on the map of the Mayan lands where we would be working for the rest of the summer."

"Brother Moody says we are on our own for dinner," Amy said as they walked to the bus. "Some members are going to the Ballet Folklorico. I'd like to go."

"If it means I can spend more time with you, I'm game," Sal said lamely. Ballet was definitely not what he had looked forward to, but ..."

Dr. Bingham called to tell Bishop Hamilton that some of the students would not be coming home until after the ballet. The bus picked them up at a restaurant near the hotel that Brother Moody had recommended. Light from evening sun surround them when the bus dropped them off at the Palace of Fine Arts. Even Sal, who admitted to no artistic taste, was astounded at the grandiose building.

"This theater," Brother Moody said, "houses the Instituto Nacional de Bellas Artes ..."

"What does that mean?" Amy whispered.

"Shhhh."

" ... consisting of art galleries and a 3500 seat theater complete with a huge pipe organ equipped with Aztec drums. You'll notice we have to go down some steps to get to the building. It wasn't built that way. The building, started in 1900, was made from such heavy Italian marble that it sunk fifteen feet into the soil."

"But how?" gasped Amy. "Remember, the city was built on a lake."

Sal nodded, sweeping his eyes around. As they walked inside he was struck with the opulence of the interior. Second and third floor galleries displayed exotic frescoes and murals. Brother Moody herded them to reserved seats. For the next two hours Sal neither said a word nor shut his eyes. The program—not ballet—was a beautifully executed and magnificently costumed series of songs, dances, and musical tableaus representing all parts of Mexico.

That night as he prepared to sleep, he knelt beside his bed in the dark. "Father in Heaven," he prayed. "I am not used to doing this, but I want to thank You for today. In my most vivid imaginings, I couldn't have foreseen all of the marvelous things I have witnessed."

Chapter 6

The bed was soft but Sal was not sleepy. He punched his pillow, but even that didn't help. He sat up, fumbled in his bag until he found his journal, and slipped down the stairs. In the study he switched on the lamp, sat at the desk, and wrote: Friday June 19. Today was an exciting day. I thought archaeology was the study of the dead. Now I feel it is a study of the living—and I am excited to be part of it. He wrote down a few more observations of Teotihuacan, the anthropology museum and the Folklorico Ballet. So much intrigued him. For a few moments he sat, his pen poised, then he wrote about his feelings—feelings of finally belonging, of being somebody, of perhaps even playing an important role in life. Back in bed, sleep came quickly, with dreaming and remembering—real and imaginary world cheerfully intermingled.

He woke refreshed and energized. A call from downstairs announced breakfast. Tammy and Sue, the Hamilton's two little daughters, had saved a place for him between them. They were cute and petite and enjoyed the attention of all the adults—and he enjoyed both of them. They reminded him of his own sisters. Breakfast was cold cereal and milk, with fruit and juice for those who wanted it. Sal had never been much of a breakfast person, but he ate two bowls of cereal with fruit on top.

The bus picked them up promptly at eight. At the hotel, Brother Moody was in the midst of another lecture. Sal found his way to the empty seat by Amy. Brother

Moody talked about Mexico City—Tenochtitlan—the city of the Aztecs.

"So far, he told about ancient civilizations in the Valley of Mexico," Amy whispered.

"Remember," Brother Moody said, "the Aztecs came late to this valley. Their history began about 1325 when, according to instructions by their prophet, they built their city on the spot where an eagle stood on a cactus with a serpent in its mouth. The cactus stood in the middle of a shallow lake. As a result, Tenochtitlan was literally built on a shallow lake bed."

Someone asked, "Yesterday, in the museum, we spent quite a bit of time discussing the Aztec calendar stone. Can you tell us about that?"

"Actually," Brother Moody replied, "the calendar used by the Aztecs was adopted from the Maya, from the Pre-Classic time period—perhaps the time of the Book of Mormon—which might suggest that the Nephites originated the Mesospheric calendar."

Amy squeezed Sal's hand.

"Yesterday you saw a model of Tenochtitlan in the museum. Today, as part of our tour of the Zocalo, or plaza area, of downtown Mexico City, you will see actual ruins of Tenochtitlan—ruins labeled as the archaeological discovery of the century. Before we go let me read one short piece about Tenochtitlan. Bernal Dia, a soldier in the army of Cortez, made this report when he first saw the fabled city of the Aztecs: *Gazing on such wonderful sights, we did not know what to say, or whether what appeared before us was real, for on the one side, on the land, there were great cities, and in the lake ever so many more, and the lake itself was crowded with canoes, and in the Causeway were many bridges at intervals, and in front of us stood the great city of Mexico...*

Through the window, Sal watched the heavy bumper to bumper traffic.

"It's awesome," breathed Amy, echoing his thoughts. "The only way to travel in Mexico City is by bus."

The bus stopped in a large, open plaza. Brother Moody picked up the microphone. "The Zocalo is not only the center of the city, but of all Mexico. All highway distances are measured from here. You will be on your own, but let me point out some of the things you may want to visit. The Cathedral is on the north, the National Palace on the east. The Palace of Justice is at the southeast corner opposite city hall. On the west are shops. Between the Cathedral and the National Palace is the archaeological excavation which I told you about. Most people call it *Templo Mayor*, the great temple of Tenochtitlan. There is a small national museum next to the excavation."

"What about lunch?" Ralph asked.

"Lunch is on your own. When you tire of sight-seeing you may want to do some shopping.

Everyone needs to be back at this spot to board the bus at five. Any questions?" Everyone rushed to get off the bus. People broke into small groups. Sal and Amy again hung close to Brother Moody. "Do you mind if we go with you, again?"

"Not at all. I'll be spending my time in the National Palace and at the Templo Mayor."

As they walked through the large central plaza, they passed hundreds of people, some having picnics, others sitting and visiting. A few sat surrounded with newspapers, pleading a special cause, while still others preached their message to anyone who would listen.

"Architecturally, this place was a near disaster area just a few years ago," Brother Moody said. "Now it has been restored to a reasonable facsimile of its former charming self. Old buildings, by decree, have been restored to their original colonial grandeur." He chuckled. "No modern chrome monstrosities are permitted here."

He pointed to the National Palace. "Note the fine baroque exterior. On that balcony," he pointed, "on

September 16, the President of Mexico rings the Liberty Bell and leads the traditional Grito."

"Liberty Bell?" Sal asked.

"Grito?" Amy exclaimed.

Brother Moody laughed. "One at a time," he said. "I'll show you the Liberty Bell inside. The Grito is a shout of freedom. Before we go into the National Palace, it might be important for you to realize that this building sits on the site of Montezuma's palace, and was at one time Cortez's residence and office."

They walked through huge wooden, carved doors. Stairs led both left and right to the second floor. "Look up." Directly above them a huge bell hung suspended. "That's the Mexican Liberty Bell. It was rung by Miguel Hidalgo on September 16, 1810, to start Mexico's battle of independence from Spain. For the Mexican people, this bell has as much significance as the Liberty Bell in Philadelphia has for the American people."

Sal's imagination crowded out the present as he thought of his people—his ancestors—fighting for their liberty. As they started up the steps, his eyes were drawn to a huge mural.

"That's a Rivera mural depicting the history of Mexico—especially the struggle of the common people," Brother Moody observed. "It's the most famous mural in all Mexico. Take your time to study this and the other murals on the balcony."

Sal leaned on the bannister and gazed at the huge picture. "It's awesome," he said. "Here is the history of my people."

Amy smiled. "At least part of your people."

As much as Sal enjoyed the mural and the National Palace, the "dig" of the Templo Mayor was more exciting. "Notice the walls," Brother Moody said. "The Aztecs built seven consecutive temples on this site. They started with a small pyramid," he pointed out the walls, "then started a new set of walls, filling in the space between with rocks and rubble. A few years alter they added still another wall, and so on until they had a huge pyramid."

"Wow! Right in the center of Mexico City," Amy said.

"Cortez destroyed Tenochtitlan in the conquest," Brother Moody said, "and then built his city on top of it."

"How did they discover this buried temple?" Sal asked.

"In 1978 a power company crew uncovered an eight ton circular stone. Excavations revealed the complete foundations of the Great Temple, as well as nineteen small stone chambers containing offerings to the gods."

"What happened to the stone?" Amy asked.

"It is housed in the National Museum." He led them down a path. "But here is a replica. The stone is considered by some to be the most important Aztec sculpture ever found."

"Yuk," Amy said, "it looks like a cut-up body."

"You are close. It really represents a dismembered moon goddess."

They wandered through museums, restaurants, and small shops. By five o'clock Sal was ready for the bus trip back to the hotel. Dinner was a quiet affair. After dinner Brother Moody gave them an orientation on the rest of the tour. "Tomorrow being Sunday, we have no planned activities. You may rest or go to church. We have made special arrangements with one of the Spanish-speaking wards. There is also an English-speaking ward. Monday morning we will have breakfast in the hotel at seven and then bus to the airport for a forty-minute flight to Oaxaca."

Sal had only a few minutes with Amy before he had to catch the bus to Hamilton's. "Amy, what are you doing tomorrow?"

"I'd like to go to church with you." "Good! Bishop Hamilton invited us to go to his ward. Can you come with us?"

"If I can catch a ride. Brother Moody!" She called.

Brother Moody came over, his smile as broad as ever.

"I'd like to go to church with Sal tomorrow at Bishop Hamilton's ward."

"No problem."

"How can I get there?"

"It's only ten thousand pesos for a taxi, or there is a regular small commuter bus which leaves every thirty minutes from here. I'll see that you get on it."

Everyone was already piled in Bishop Hamilton's van when Amy arrived the next morning. Sal had a few nervous moments, wondering if she would make it in time. Bishop Hamilton had left earlier for Bishop's meeting. Sebastian, the Chauffeur, drove them to church. The chapel itself sat back on a small lot, nothing spectacular, but the people were wonderful. Everyone wanted to be introduced, from small children to the aged.

Bishop Hamilton, flanked by his native Mexican counselors, presided over the late-starting meeting. Sal glanced around at the many empty seats.

The bishop announced the opening song. Amy whispered, "The piano is out of tune."

Sal nodded.

Enthusiastic singing made up for the out-of-tune piano. The group was small but they sang *con gusto*—with much enthusiasm. People drifted in during the singing, filling the small chapel.

Sal thought to himself, *What a happy people.* Most of the ward members came from very humble circumstances, but still they seemed happy and had a special spirit about them. In class, he was impressed with the Sunday School teacher—a young man, no older than himself, but one who seemed well-learned in the Church. Sal kept a running translation to Amy, so she wouldn't miss what was said.

The teacher wrote on the blackboard, OBEDIENCIA.

Amy nudged him, "Obedience?"

He smiled and nodded.

As the lesson progressed, the teacher said, and Sal translated, "David and Saul had their Goliath. But each of us has our own Goliath. His giant size depends upon the extent of our thoughts and sins. We can cut him down to size by reducing our sinful thoughts."

He wrote on the board:
PENSAMIENTO (THOUGHT)=
TENTACION' (TEMPTATION)=
PECADO (SIN)=
MIEDO (FEAR)=
ARREPENTIMIENTO (REPENTANCE) O (OR)
PECADO (MORE SIN)

"God has to be the central figure of our lives and our thoughts," the teacher said.

After Sunday School Sal introduced himself to the teacher. "No tengo el gusto de conocerle,"

"Me llamo, Rafael," "My name is Raphael."

"I really enjoyed the lesson," Sal said.

Rafael looked pleased. "I am a student, learning to be an attorney."

He attended Priesthood and sacrament meeting. RaNae took Amy with her to Relief Society. But Sal spent most of his time thinking of the Sunday School teacher's words: "God has to be the central figure in our lives and thoughts." That saying filled his thoughts as they drove home.

He did notice great contrasts in how people lived. Reforma, a beautiful street, had an island in the middle filled with grass and trees. But side streets were heaped with trash and garbage. Fine expensive lined Reforma. Homes in some areas seemed to be nothing more than shacks.

After dinner, Sister Hamilton announced, "I need to go visiting teaching. Would either of you like to go with me?"

Both Sal and Amy jumped at the chance. They wanted to see how the Mexican people lived.

The home they visited was in a poor area of town. Homes joined homes, wall-to-wall, with no yards for children to play in. Children played in the dirt street. The home, though small and cramped for the size of family, was clean. Sister Hamilton introduced them to Rosa and her three children. Rosa's parents, not members of the Church, also lived in the cramped home. Rosa brought them a mint tea and they sipped while Sister Hamilton visited. One of the children, a little boy of about two, climbed on Sal's lap and stayed there until they left. *There is dirt in the streets*, Sal thought, *but I have never known such a warm, friendly people. If my grandfather had not sneaked across the Rio Grande into the United States, this might be the kind of home I was reared in.*

He was quiet on the ride back to the Hamilton's.

"A penny for your thoughts," Amy quipped.

"I have never seen such poverty," he said, still watching out the window of the van. "As poor as our people are in my home town, they are rich in comparison."

Sister Hamilton joined the conversation. "There is a great contrast. The wealthy are able to buy anything. Markets are filled with meats, fruit, vegetables, and flowers."

"And the poor?" Amy asked.

"The poor eke out a living and live on tortillas and whatever else they can purchase at the outdoor markets."

"Salvador!"

He buried his face in the pillow but someone continued shaking him. "*Salvador, son las siete y media. Es hora de partir.*"

Groggily Sal looked up into the frantic eyes of Guadalupe, the Hamilton maid.

"Where is everyone?"

"*No le se'.*"

He slipped on his clothes and ran downstairs. The house seemed deserted. The kitchen was empty, with exception of the dirty dishes still on the table and bar. The Hamilton family was all gone—and apparently, so were his companions and Dr. Bingham. Then he remembered Dr. Bingham had stayed with some friends.

Panic seized him. Quickly he brushed his teeth, slicked his hair and threw everything into his suitcase. Guadalupe stood by, wringing her hands nervously. He glanced at his watch: 7:50. The bus was supposed to pick them up at 7:30. Why hadn't someone awakened him earlier? No breakfast and no shower.

"Gracias, Guadalupe," he called over his shoulder as he ran to the front gate; no one there, either. He remembered the taxi stand on the corner—two houses down. He ran to the dispatcher,

"Holiday Inn Crowne Plaza, por favor," he cried. The dispatcher pointed to the first cab, an ancient Volkswagen, in a row of three. Sal jumped in the cab and again cried, "Holiday Inn Crown Plaza, por favor."

A short taxi ride and 10,000 pesos later, he stood at the front door of the Holiday Inn. With relief he recognized several of the tour members. At least the tour had not departed. He hurried inside. Amy stood at the check-out desk.

"Good morning, Sal," she said brightly. "I didn't expect you so early."

"Why not?" Sal said, prepared to tell her about his close call of missing the flight.

"At breakfast Brother Moody announced our flight to Oaxaca had been delayed. Dr. Bingham said that since the flight was late, he thought he'd let you boys sleep in an extra half- hour, so he called Bishop Hamilton and told him to let you sleep."

Sal was still shaken. "But what about the others?"

"Next."

Amy whispered, "Just a minute," and stepped to the desk. Sal looked around. None of his "dig" mates were here. What had happened to them? He didn't know whether to tell Amy about the wild taxi ride or not. While he waited, he stepped back to the front door. The bus pulled up with the "dig" crew.

"Where did you come from?" a kid named Whitt yelled.

"How come you didn't wake me up?" Sal asked angrily.

"Whoa," Whitt said. "Take it easy. We decided to pick up the rest of the crew and get you on the way back."

"Besides, we left word for Guadalupe to wake you at 7:30," John Brudman, another dig member said.

Amy had joined them. "What's all the fuss?"

"Just a little mix-up," Sal grumbled. "A mix-up that stressed me out and made me 10,000 pesos poorer." He told the whole story to Amy on the bus ride to the airport.

She didn't sympathize with him at all, but laughed and enjoyed his obvious discomfiture. "Besides," she said, "ten thousand pesos is only a little over three dollars."

"It's three dollars I didn't have to spend. Besides, I didn't even get a chance to say a final goodbye and thank-you to Bishop and Sister Hamilton."

Chapter 7

The DC-9 rose quickly into the air, exposing the heavy haze and smog in the Valley of Mexico. Sal looked out the tiny window trying to discern objects on the ground through the solid- gray overcast.

"You mean we've been breathing that stuff?" Bill Hestler, another "dig" mate said.

"Mexico City has the worst smog problem in the world," Dr. Bingham said. "And right now, with over twenty-million people in the city, there seems to be no solution."

"Look," Amy said excitedly, pointing out the window. Ahead of the wing, rising as it were right out of the clouds and the smog, two beautiful cone-shaped mountains stretched high into the sky, catching the glory of the morning sun. Tendrils of smoke came from the taller cone, and though it was mid-summer, its top was draped in snow.

"Popocateptl and Ixtaccihuatl," Dr. Bingham said.

"Popo what?" Sal asked.

Dr. Bingham laughed. "That's what most people call it, just plain 'Popo.' Popocateptl means 'smoking mountain'. The other volcano, Ixtaccihuatl, or Ixta, means sleeping lady."

"Like Timpanogas," Amy remarked.

"And with a similar story."

Amy, always the romantic, clasped her hands and said, "Please tell us."

Dr. Bingham needed no urging. "Popocatepetl, a warrior chief, was madly in love with Ixtaccihuatl. But the emperor, Ixta's father, offered her in marriage to any chieftain who would bring him victory in an impending battle. During the battle a rival suitor sent word that Popo was killed in battle. Ixta, not wishing to marry anyone but Popo, sickened and died. When he found his sweetheart had died, Popo was desolate. He built a smaller pyramid where he buried his beloved, then built a larger one for himself where he could keep eternal watch over her."

"What a sad but beautiful story," Amy said.

"And one captured in legend in many countries of the world," Brother Moody said. "Similar stories were found often in Greek mythology."

Sal, though interested in the discussion, felt really sleepy. He reclined his seat, grabbed a pillow, and slept. Sun coming in his window awakened him. He looked out at the strange cloud formations. A high layer blanketed the sky, but below, rows of clouds lined up like furrows in a field of corn, clouds maintaining straight lines with clear space between where Sal could look down upon the green of the forest far below.

A bus waited at the airport. "Oaxaca, pronounced Wa HA ca," Dr. Bingham said, "is a popular tourist center. The valley sits at about 5000 feet elevation, which gives it a pleasant year-round climate. Monte Alban, considered the most important archaeological site, is only one of many. Archaeologists identified over two-hundred sites in this valley."

As if on cue, Brother Moody picked up the discussion, "Monte Alban was a Zapotec city built in Book of Mormon times."

Dr. Bingham added, "The Zapotec ruins date from about 500 BC to 750 AD. From my research, I believe the Oaxaca Valley played a vital role in the development of the civilizations of the Book of Mormon . Because of its location, northwest of the Isthmus of Tehuantepec, it could qualify as the land of Moron in the early Jaredite or

Olmec history. After the arrival of the Mulekites, the Oaxaca Valley may have been one of the areas they settled.

"The second period of time represented by Monte Alban has been dated as 180 BC. Archaeologists indicate settlers arrived from Guatemala or Chiapas. This coincides with the time period when Mosiah led a Nephite group from the Land of Nephi down to the City of Zarahemla. I feel some of that group continued north to the Oaxaca Valley. Archaeological evidence convinces me that Nephites abounded in the Oaxaca Valley."

Brother Moody interrupted. "We're almost there and there are several things I want you to pay particular attention to. First, note that Monte Alban was built on a hilltop, just like Jerusalem or Bethlehem. Second, visit the small museum near Monte Alban. There you will find carbon- dating paralleling Book of Mormon dates, and finally, note the stone monuments named *the Dancers*. We will discuss their significance later."

Sal was not satisfied. "You said the dates of Monte Alban parallel the Book of Mormon "

"That's true," Dr. Bingham was patient. "On-site evidence indicates the area might have been home for the early Jaredite culture. Other archaeological evidence leads us to assume the Oaxaca Valley was settled by segments of the Mulekites from the sixth to the third Centuries BC."

"How do you explain that?" Sal persisted.

Dr. Bingham shrugged and looked out the window at the lush valley. "There is little hard data available," he said, "but archaeologists almost unanimously agree the Olmecs were influential in Monte Alban's development."

"Oh," Amy said, "and the Olmecs were the Jaredites."

"Right," Brother Moody smiled, "and the Book of Mormon tells us the Mulekites landed in Jaredite territory."

"So the Jaredites would have influenced the Mulekites."

The stopping of the bus interrupted the discussion. Sal and Amy hung close to Brother Moody, not wanting to miss a word.

"In its glory," he said, "the vast archaeological city occupied a group of hills 25 miles square. Only Monte Alban has been reconstructed."

Sal was amazed—the word for the ruins was "awesome." The reconstructed pyramids and buildings were on a much smaller scale than the pyramids at Teotihuacan and of a much different architecture, but Monte Alban also had a different feel to it. From their commanding location in the plaza the valley's panorama opened before them. Modern Indian dancers, in exotic feather headdresses and costumes, jumped and leaped in the plaza. Vendors—young children to those wrinkled with age—cried their wares: jade carvings, silver ornaments and jewelry.

"This is the 'Building of the Dancers,'" Brother Moody said, stopping before a large temple. "The carvings called the dancers represent a significant archaeological find." He pointed at several stone monuments engraved with figures of people. "Note that some of the figures appear to be in ballerina-type dancing positions—therefore the name. Note some figures are obviously nude. Perhaps the nudeness represented some form of captivity, such as the Jewish captivity by the Babylonians. He pointed out several other monuments. "Notice these two monuments depict figures who appear to be blind, crawling on their hands and knees. From Biblical history you will recall the Babylonians captured Jerusalem, and blinded King Zedekiah after killing his sons."

Sal busily scribbled notes. There was so much material—most of it still confusing.

On the bus, Sal and Amy compared notes. They contrasted earlier buildings with those built after the time of Christ. "What interested me," Amy said, "are the changes made after 200 AD."

"Dr. Bingham said special places were built where dignitaries could observe the ball games, and the tombs of the priests became more important and spacious," Sal agreed.

"That parallels the time in the Book of Mormon when the people became dominated by a priestly class."

Sal just nodded again, and read through his notes. I must be thick-headed, he thought. I wish I could see the connection as clearly as Amy. He was relieved to get back on the bus. There was so much to learn, and even more to try to understand. He took Amy's hand as the bus traveled down the mountain. "Amy, I still have difficulty separating truth from theory."

"I'm not sure either," she squeezed his hand. "That's what we are here to find out."

"All this speculation about the tie-in between the archaeological evidence and the Book of Mormon ..." he let the thought dangle.

"But you can see the possibility exists," Amy said patiently.

"Oh, sure," he said. "But it is still only speculation."

Most of the four-hour bus ride to Tehuantepec was downhill. The narrow roads seemed hardly wide enough for a car, let alone the bus. When other cars passed it looked for sure as if they were going to hit. As they dropped in elevation, mountain brush turned to palm and banana trees, and other tropical plants. Skinny brindle-white cows grazed in open spots in the jungle; small, white birds perched on their backs. Colorful parrots flew across the road. Farmers walked along the road, long, wicked-looking machetes on their shoulders.

The buses finally stopped at nine that night. The hotel, a long, low, white building, sat back from the road. On the front, raised black letters proclaimed, "Hotel Calli."

"Everyone out," Dr. Bingham said, cheerfully. "This is our home for tonight."

"Be careful of the water," Brother Moody added. "Drink only the bottled water the hotel provides—use it even for brushing your teeth."

Heat and humidity—after riding on an air-conditioned bus—broiled the skin. Within moments, Sal's shirt was wringing wet. "Is there a swimming pool?" he asked the clerk.

"Si, Senor," she said, pointing to the rear.

After checking in, Sal called to Amy. "I'll see you in the pool as soon as you can change."

The pool refreshed him. The water did not seem too clean, but its coolness made up for sanitation. Sal swam leisurely back and forth as he waited for Amy. "I wouldn't dive in," he called as she finally arrived.

She looked at the water hesitantly.

"Come on in," he called, splashing her. "Just be careful not to drink any water."

"I don't think we should even talk, for fear of getting it in our mouths," she shuddered.

"Aw, it's not that bad. Besides, it's cool."

Nighttime brought some relief from the heat, but not the humidity. The group ate dinner in an open dining area, where a breeze from the sea made it somewhat bearable. Sal ordered Camaron Relleno, stuffed shrimp. Amy teased him. "You eat that as if you never expected to be able to eat again."

"You never know," he said, putting another tasty morsel in his mouth. "None of us know what tomorrow will bring."

Sal woke in a sweat. His body, under the light sheet, felt clammy. He kicked off the bed covers and lay on top in his underwear. Heat and humidity still smothered him, even this early in the morning. He had never felt heat so oppressive. He gave up and finally got up. The shower, a shared one down the hall, cooled and tingled his skin, but Sal was still wringing wet when he dressed.

At breakfast, Amy was very thoughtful. "Sal, I think it would be a good idea if each night we would go over our notes and see if we have any points of agreement."

"Fine with me," Sal said. He smiled. "In fact," he teased, "any way I can spend more time with you will be muy bueno." He took her hand in both of his and, without taking his eyes from hers, kissed it gently.

Amy looked around, embarrassed. "Please, Sal."

Brother Moody interrupted his little game. "Listen up, everyone," he said. "Before we start, I would like to do a little map study with you." He unfolded a map of Southern Mexico and Central America. "You are at the center of Mesoamerica." He pointed to their location on the Isthmus of Tehuantepec. "In this ancient land, natural boundaries played a major role in the divisions of the cultures. Mountains or bodies of water formed common boundaries in the land. The Isthmus of Tehuantepec has long been a natural dividing line. The Book of Mormon speaks often of the narrow neck of land." He looked around the room. "Do any of you have your scriptures?" Hands went up. "Turn to verse 32 of Alma 22."

"What was that reference again," Bill asked.

"Alma, chapter 22, verse 32. Amy, will you read it?"

"...there being a small neck of land between the land northward and the land southward."

"I always assumed the Isthmus of Panama was the narrow neck of land," Bill said.

"At one time in the Church, many people assumed the same thing. However, archaeological evidence doesn't support that choice. Most Mormon scholars have concluded that the Isthmus of Tehuantepec is the narrow neck of land."

Sal had heard enough about "evidence" without seeing any. "What kind of evidence?"

"I appreciate your asking," Brother Moody replied. "For one thing, between here and Vera Cruz has been identified by archaeologists as the heartland of the ancient Olmec culture. Since the founding of the Church, all scholars—including Joseph Smith—came to the conclusion that Mesoamerica was the location of Book of Mormon culture. The Isthmus of Panama has few archaeological remains of any kind. Thirdly, the highest density of population in ancient America was concentrated on both sides of this Isthmus. The fourth, and perhaps most important, criterion is that this area was the only geographical area in the entire New World where a system of writing was regularly employed before the coming of the Europeans."

Dr. Bingham broke in. "North of us is Oaxaca, with its ancient cultures. On the Gulf side are Vera Cruz and sites of countless ruins. Southeast of us is the central depression of Chiapas—a large basin which we feel was the land of Zarahemla. I'm not here to impress you with my knowledge, but from my thirty-five year study of the archaeology of this area, I am convinced that the Isthmus of Tehuantepec is the Narrow Neck of Land spoken of in the Book of Mormon."

Brother Moody looked around to see if there were any more questions.

Sal shrugged. It certainly sounded believable.

"Some of this information will come as we travel," Brother Moody suggested. "Today, we'll check out of the hotel, travel for several hours through the narrow land bridge above Tehuantepec, have a brief rest stop at Tonala—about midway between here and Tapachula—and then continue to Tapachula located on the Guatemala border. We'll be in the bus for about six hours, so there will be plenty of time for questions."

Corn fields covered the hillsides above Tehuantepec. Sapling trees, living fence posts, marched single file up and over the hills. Sal wondered how crops could be planted, tended, and harvested in such steep places. In the valleys, lush tropical vegetation—date palms, banana trees, and coconut palms—grew to the edge of the road.

The bus stopped at a small village. "This will be a toilet stop," Brother Moody said. "You will only have a few moments, so please hurry." Amy and most of the women left the bus.

Sal had Dr. Bingham almost to himself. Hungry for information, he asked. "Dr. Bingham, what are some of the geographic requirements of the narrow neck of land?"

The professor sat on the arm of a seat. "Good question, Sal. From a geographic point of view, the Book of Mormon is quite explicit. The narrow neck had to be wide enough that the explorers sent out by King Limhi could pass through it without realizing it was an isthmus. On the other hand, it had to be narrow enough that, as the Book of Mormon describes it, it was only the distance of a day and a half's journey for a Nephite, on the line Bountiful and the Land Desolation, from the east to the west sea. Of course, we don't know how long the 'day's travel' might have been, but the total, straight-line width from Atlantic shore to Pacific lagoon edge is 120 miles.

"One of the interesting things," he continued, "which most people don't realize, is that the Book of Mormon story took place in a small geographical area—an area measured in hundreds, not thousands, of miles." He laughed. "Even students of the Book of Mormon who accept the Isthmus of Tehuantepec as the narrow neck of land still differ about other geographical Book of Mormon lands." Dr. Bingham became serious again. "The main point is, the Book of Mormon account actually did take place somewhere. We who believe the book are confident that there were indeed real places where real Nephis and Almas did the real things the book says they did."

"Thanks," Sal said, slightly overwhelmed. He got up and walked out of the bus to stretch his legs. There was still a long line-up of women in front of the small toilet building. He climbed back in the bus and wrote a few notes of what Dr. Bingham had said. He highlighted and double- underlined real places and real Nephis and

Almas. Amy finally got back on board. "What took you so long?" he chided.

"I don't even want to talk about it," she said testily.

Sal dozed intermittently on the long bus ride. When awake, he looked at the scenery—if you could call it scenery—which didn't vary. Little ranches, with stands of trees and haciendas, lay on both sides of the highway. To the east, a range of low mountains, brushy and steep, thrust into the sky. Westward, though he couldn't see it, was the Pacific Ocean. The whole coastal plain looked to be less than ten miles wide.

Tonala turned out to be a sleepy Mexican village with the typical Pemex petrol station and several tourist shops selling T-shirts and pottery. A small stream meandered through the town and Sal was intrigued to see many young-looking Indian women washing clothes on the rocks. Children played around the bridge.

As the bus pulled into Tapachula, Sal glanced at his watch—2:00 in the afternoon. Tall palm trees lined the highway. Orchards—straight rows of some kind of trees—extended into the distance. Stepping out of the air-conditioned bus was like stepping into a blast furnace. Tapachula was even hotter than Tehuantepec. Carrying his and Amy's luggage, he stepped into the open-air lobby of the Hotel Loma Real. The change from outside was dramatic. Sal looked around. The hotel, located on a hilltop, was surrounded by lush vegetation. Flower gardens and lawns were carved from the jungle. Brightly-colored birds chattered and argued. Lizards climbed the walls

Chapter 8

A steep, muddy road led to the ruins of Izapa. The small minivan bounced through the ruts, throwing people in each others' laps. No one could talk. When they arrived at the site of the ruins, Sal shook his head, disappointed. There was little to see: a cow pasture with a few stones in it, and mounds that Brother Moody called temples and pyramids.

Amy could see his disappointment. "Come on, Sal," she chided. "Brother Moody and Dr. Bingham wouldn't have brought us here unless it was important."

Swatting at flies, he grabbed her hand and hurried to catch up. Brother Moody said, "Some scholars theorized that the Tapachula area is the site of the landing of Lehi, the Land of First Inheritance."

Sal, his irritation showing, asked, "So why this place rather than some other?"

Brother Moody was patient. "Izapa is an ancient ceremonial center. From 600 BC to 350 AD, it seems to have been the largest and most important center on the Pacific Coast, serving both civil and religious functions."

Dr. Bingham added, "The Izapa culture is located within the Maya geographical area. Yet, archaeologically, Izapa represents a separate and unique culture. The main development of Izapa culture parallels the Book of Mormon time period."

"But strictly theory," Sal groused to Amy.

"Shhh."

"In the late 1940's archaeologists discovered Stela 5, which has been given the name of the 'Tree-of-Life' stone.

Field work has been conducted here by Brigham Young University since the early fifties."

Dr. Bingham was still talking, "A Latter-Day-Saint archaeologist named Garth Norman spent years studying the Izapa civilization. He produced some interesting correlations between Izapa and the old world culture."

"For instance?" Sal asked, still feeling irritated.

"Well, for one thing," Dr. Bingham stated, "Norman discovered that the 'cubit' was the principal form of measurement at Izapa." He looked around at the group. "Why might that be significant?"

Whitt Lavell answered, "The cubit was the standard of measurement of ancient Israel."

"Scholars wondered how it got here," Dr. Bingham continued, "but if this is where Lehi landed, a few years after he left Jerusalem, then there should be no question about its origin. If, Izapa, in reality, is the Land of First Inheritance of Lehi and his people, located as it is along the Pacific corridor which leads to the Isthmus of Tehuantepec, then the area certainly fulfills the requirement of the Lord's covenant people."

"Izapa is the crossroads of the Americas," Brother Moody interrupted. "You'll notice that east of here the terrain gets pretty rugged. During Book of Mormon times, the terrain dictated that anyone traveling by land from north to south had to pass through the Isthmus. Upon arriving on the Pacific side, the traveler could choose between two routes, the upper route through the Chiapas depression and on into the Peten area of Guatemala, or the coastal route which took the traveler through the heart of the Izapa country." He looked around at the tour group. "Let me ask another question. "The population declined to almost nothing by 350 A.D. Can anyone guess why?"

There was no response. Finally Amy timorously raised her hand. "Is that when the Nephites gave up the Land Southward to the Lamanites."

"Good!" Brother Moody said, winking at her.

Dr. Bingham said, "Izapa may actually be the city of Judea mentioned in the Book of Mormon, a very strategic location near the Isthmus of Tehuantepec." He turned and pointed to the low-lying mounds. "These earthen mounds, the eroded remnants of platforms faced with natural rounded stones, but originally covered with clay or lime plaster, form a maze of courts and plazas, and may represent the most significant Book of Mormon culture we have found."

Sal looked around. *What significant culture?* he asked himself. *A few mounds and a few monuments?*

By this time, the tour group was in the middle of the field, surrounded by various upright stones. Dr. Bingham knelt beside one, protected by a small gable roof. "This is Stela 5. We believe this stela represents Lehi's vision of the Tree of Life." He pointed out various carvings, and attempted to relate them to Lehi's dream. "Stela 5 has been carbon-dated to sometime between 300 B.C. and 50 B.C."

"And the rest?" Whitt asked.

"All of the stela and most of the pyramids were carved or constructed between 300 B.C. and 350 A.D." He shook his head sadly. "Stela 5 is deteriorating each year here in the open. Our attempts to have it put in a museum have so far been unsuccessful."

The bus ride back to Tapachula seemed even bumpier. Sal hung on and thought about what the two professors had said. How could such a plain-looking area yield so much archaeological information? *Dummy!* he said to himself. *I guess I have much to learn about archaeology.*

After lunch, they checked out of the hotel and boarded the large, air-conditioned bus for the journey to Guatemala City. "The Guatemala border is only about five minutes," Brother Moody said. "Guatemala City is another five-hours."

Sal put his arm around Amy. He snuggled his head against hers, and soon dozed. Roar of the bus motor and gears scraping as the driver geared down woke Sal. Smell of diesel fumes almost gagged him. He reached in his back pocket for his handkerchief, covered his nostrils, and looked around. Most everyone on the bus was asleep. Amy, long legs tucked beneath her, was curled up on her seat. Long, blond hair framed her face. He ran his fingers gently through it.

Outside, the night was dark with no moon. He could tell they were climbing, but he could see nothing outside except occasional lights of a sleepy village or restaurant alongside the road. Through the windshield he finally saw a road sign illuminated by the headlights: *Ciudad de Guatemala, 24 kilometers.* He gazed unseeing through the window. Thoughts crowded his mind. *Dr. Bingham and Brother Moody seem so sure. They have studied this setting for years. Who am I to challenge them? What right do I have to question their information?* He gently pulled Amy to him until her head rested on his shoulder. A soft moan escaped her throat.

The bus, after traveling through the suburbs, turned down a beautiful avenue, well-lighted, with a strip of trees down its center. Amy woke, yawned, and looked around. Large, luxury hotels crowded every corner of the thorofare. Cars and trucks filled the avenue; sidewalks teemed with pedestrians. The street sign said, *Avenida Reforma.* The bus turned onto a side street and stopped in front of a hotel. The brightly-lighted sign said, Hotel El Dorado.

After the back-country hotels they had stayed in the last few nights, Sal was amazed at the affluence of the El Dorado. Dark wood paneling and frescoed ceilings decorated lobby and hallways. Soft, recessed lighting hinted at quiet elegance. Directories pointed out restaurants, tennis courts, swimming pools, steam baths, and gymnasiums. He hoped he would have time to work out during their stay.

Little was said by his roommates. They brushed their teeth and fell into bed. Sal lay awake thinking. *Here I am,* an American from a small town in New Mexico—a transplanted Mexican—in Guatemala City. Tomorrow we will visit more ruins. Dr. Bingham and Brother Moody will present more evidence that the ruins are part of Book of Mormon times. Shall I accept everything or continue to question? With that thought, he fell asleep.

At breakfast Brother Moody was his usual, cheerful self. "Today we start with a visit to the Guatemala National Museum of Archaeology and Ethnology. The museum has an extensive collection of stelae, pottery, and other artifacts from the time-period of the Book of Mormon. If our hypothesis is correct, somewhere in this valley is the site of the Land of Nephi. Nephi brought his people here after leaving the Land of their First Inheritance, possibly Izapa, where we were yesterday. The ruins of Kaminaljuyu is possibly the remains of the City of Nephi."

The bus ride to the museum was short. They passed under a high, colonial aqueduct, partly in ruins. The museum was modern, with plaster models of archaeological sites. Sal and Amy followed Dr. Bingham into a room with an extensive collection of artifacts from Kaminaljuyu.

"I still wish they would put the descriptions in English," Amy complained. "I can't read any of them."

"I'll be your guide," Sal said, taking her by the arm. "It will give me something to do—to read them for you."

After lunch they visited the archaeological zone of Kaminaljuyu. Sal was again disappointed. He had expected some regular pyramids, or at least some reconstruction work. Instead, the ruins consisted of dozens of low mounds and what resembled caved-in basements.

"Kaminaljuyu flourished within the limits of what is now Guatemala City," Dr. Bingham said. "Sadly, during the last century most of the hundreds of mounds that once made up the great ceremonial center have been destroyed to make way for housing and commercial development. Some treasures of pottery and jewelry were recovered and placed in the National Museum, but private collectors carried off an untold amount."

They walked between what looked like small hills. Dr. Bingham picked up a shard of pottery. "These mounds, covered over with dirt and vegetation, are what remain of temple platforms. The temples, in an area a mile square, were built around patios and plazas. Most were constructed over burial sites, from which came the name Kaminaljuyu: 'Hill of the Dead.' Archaeologists date the founding of the city between 1000 B.C. and 600 B.C. As you know, that ties closely to the date when Nephi left his brothers and took his people into the mountains. The people who inhabited the city were skilled at sculpture and pottery, and used glyph writing."

"Were any metal implements found?" Sal asked.

"Interestingly enough," Dr. Bingham replied, "about the only metal objects found were of gold or gold alloys."

"With all of these mounds just waiting, why don't we see any digs here?" Amy asked.

"Lack of money. There is a wealth of information here just waiting to tell its story."

"Notice also," Brother Moody added, "that Kaminaljuyu was situated on a broad plain. Most later Mayan cities in Guatemala were located on hilltops or narrow canyons which were defensible. That would indicate that the era when Kaminaljuyu thrived was a time of peace."

"That wasn't really the case at the time of King Noah," Bill said.

"True," Brother Moody admitted, "but it was true at the time the city was built. It wasn't until after the Lamanites discovered where Nephi and his people had gone that conflicts began."

Sal looked up from his notes. "Were other native people already here in the valley when Nephi came?" he asked.

Brother Moody laughed. "That question could have a sting to it," he said. "Mormons are not used to the idea that people other than Lehi's immediate descendants were on the Book of Mormon scene. However, abundant archaeological evidence indicates that such people were indeed present."

"Which means," Dr. Bingham added, "that Nephi and his people dominated a native population already scattered throughout the land."

"Remember the Book of Mormon does not claim to be a history of this or any geographical area," Brother Moody said. "It is only what it claims to be, a second witness of Jesus Christ."

Sal was thoughtful on the way back to the hotel.

"A penny for your thoughts," Amy volunteered. He shook his head.

"Just trying to sort out all that I'm learning."

Everyone dressed for dinner. Cleaning up was a welcome change from traveling grubbies, especially for the women. Guatemala City's pleasant temperature also contributed to a feeling of well-being in Sal. They walked from the hotel to a restaurant called *El Rodeo*. The decor, rustic and woody, resembled many steak houses in New Mexico.

"The steaks are excellent here," Brother Moody said, "and in large portions. When it's aged and cooked right, Guatemalan beef is marvelous. You will also notice the menu features typical Guatemalan food and seafood." He smiled. "Your meal is included in your tour package, so eat what you want."

Barbecuing meat filled the cafe with succulent aromas, making Sal's mouth water in anticipation. There was no question in his mind—he ordered a medium-rare steak. Amy wanted to try the *'typical'* menu. She ordered a marinated, native meat dish cooked on an open grill. The waitress brought small tacos and finger-sized enchiladas as appetizers. Sal ate with enjoyment, telling Amy, between mouthfuls, about his conclusions.

"Perhaps it's the Spirit telling me," he said, "but everything I'm hearing and reading makes me feel the Book of Mormon really could be true."

His conversation was interrupted as the waitress returned with steaming meat dishes, garlanded with mushrooms, in a hot, garlic-buttery sauce. Sal smacked his lips in anticipation. "I've never eaten food like this," he said, as he sliced off a piece of the pink meat and plopped it into his mouth. "Mom cooked meat, but she believed it had to be black to be done."

Amy smiled at Sal's enthusiasm. She had never seen him happier. "Did your mother cook Mexican food?" She took a small bite, savoring its subtle flavor.

"All the time," he grimaced. "But I was too Americanized. I liked junk foods." He speared another piece of meat on his fork, rolling it in the sauce. He chewed it slowly, obviously enjoying it. "I didn't realize meat could taste so good."

"So," she said, "why this sudden conversion?"

Sal sat up, surprised she wasn't more enthusiastic about his "conversion." He shrugged. "I guess Brother Moody and Dr. Bingham convinced me. Every place we have been the archaeological evidence seems to point to the fact that it is true."

"I didn't think you would give in so easily," Amy put down her fork and looked across the table at him. "You seemed harder to convince than that," she mused, a twinkle in her eyes.

"But," Sal said, at a loss for words. "I thought you would be pleased."

"I will be pleased when I am convinced that you have a testimony of the Book of Mormon" Amy said seriously. "I don't believe in 'death-bed' conversions."

"Death-bed?"

"It's the same thing, conversion for convenience."

"But, Amy," he pleaded. "I'm serious. Intellectually, I really believe the Book of Mormon is true. I thought you would be happy."

She deliberately took a napkin and wiped the corners of her mouth, reached for her compact and reapplied her lipstick. Carefully putting it away, she commented. "I'll accept your conversion, if it's still with you, when you return to Provo after your 'dig.'"

Sal was quiet during the rest of the meal. In his head, his thoughts were, How does one ever understand women and their thought processes?

Chapter 9

Friday morning dawned bright and cool. Sal went for a jog before breakfast, enjoying the early morning. Few pedestrians walked along Reforma, though traffic was heavy. He had a quick shower, then hurried to meet Amy in the lobby for breakfast.

"Good morning," she said brightly. "You almost missed breakfast." She looked as fresh as the morning—all dew and flowers. She took his arm and led him to a table. "Where have you been?"

"I went for a little run," he said, still smarting a little from her lack of understanding.

The waiter placed a bowl of fruit in front of them, then asked for their order.

"I'll have an omelette," Sal said without looking at the menu, "and orange juice to drink."

"I'll just have the orange juice and fruit," Amy said. She waited for the waiter to leave. "I'm sorry if what I said last night hurt your feelings," she said, looking at Sal with widened eyes.

"It made no difference," Sal lied, peeling a banana and taking a bite. "I just always wonder if you care about me at all." He swallowed. "I don't even know if you'll want to marry me even when I get a testimony of the Book of Mormon."

She reached across the table and took his hand. "Of course I care about you. And, when the time comes, if things work out, I will want to marry you."

Sal chewed in silence, almost choking on the banana. He didn't know what to say.

"It's easy to accept convictions of others," Amy said, filling in the conversational void, "but that isn't good enough. I realize you have to find out for yourself. At first I felt upset at you for questioning everything. Now I feel it is all right. You cannot accept Brother Moody's testimony, or even Dr. Bingham's evidence that the Book of Mormon is true. Not even your so-called logical testimony will do."

Sal started to speak but she interrupted him.

"Sal, your testimony can be partly based on the evidence you are finding but eventually it must come from your heart." She looked down at her plate, tears suddenly welling in her eyes. Her mascara smeared. She looked up. "I do love you, Sal, and I hope someday to marry you."

Brother Moody came by the table. "Good morning," he said pleasantly. "Ready for today's excursion?"

"Sure," Sal said easily, eyeing Amy.

"Wear light clothing and a hat," Brother Moody said. "The sun at Tikal is usually strong, though you can escape it for a while by ducking under a tree or into a temple. Also, wear shoes with non-slip soles for climbing temples."

"Are the temples very high?" Amy asked, her head turned as she fixed her makeup.

"If you are afraid of heights, they are high," Moody laughed. "Getting up the long flights of steps is no problem, but getting down might be."

Brother Moody talked all the way on the bus ride to the airport. "The Peten, or jungle, to which we are now going, represents the lowland area of Guatemala. The Maya ruins of Tikal date from about 600 BC to 900 AD. The ruins represent one of the most massive population centers in Mesoamerica. Over 3000 separate structures, spread over ten square miles, have been analyzed at Tikal. Much restoration work has been done."

"Is Tikal a Book of Mormon city?" Sal asked. The bus was climbing up a mesa to the airport. Sal listened while looking out the window at the city laid out in all directions below.

Brother Moody turned to Dr. Bingham. Dr. Bingham smiled and answered. "According to the archaeological evidence, the Mulekites and Olmecs were the first settlers of Tikal." He was about to go on when the bus stopped at the passenger entrance to the terminal. "We'll continue our discussion later."

Sal anticipated what Dr. Bingham would say. He had seen pictures of Tikal in the *National Geographic*. Would he be disappointed at the actual site? Would Tikal prove to be another city like exciting Teotihuacan? Or more like the pallid ruins of Kaminaljuyu?

The flight to Tikal took only thirty-five minutes. Dr. Bingham used the intercom. "We date the site of Tikal to about 600 BC," he said, "but no buildings date that far back. The Maya destroyed old structures and used the materials for new buildings. We've found pottery shards that date to several hundred years before Christ. The Preclassic Maya period has not been thoroughly explored in Tikal. More emphasis has been put on the Classic period, which starts about 200 AD."

"When was the site abandoned?" Whitt asked.

"Most Mesoamerican sites, including Tikal, were abandoned between 750 and 900 AD. The Mayan population on both sides of the Isthmus of Tehuantepec numbered in the millions. After the great apostasy in 200 AD, the Nephites, or members of the Church of Christ, represented a small minority as compared to the overall populace. The Maya Classic Period, or period when Tikal was at its height, was really the period of the great apostasy in Mesoamerica. The people developed a massive building program and literally built gods unto themselves."

"When did human sacrifices begin?" John asked.

"We have no evidence of human sacrifices at Tikal."

"So what we'll see in Tikal is mostly post-Book of Mormon?" Sal asked.

"Yes, though some Mormons have tried to label everything Maya as Book of Mormon."

Brother Moody laughed. "When Mormon tourists go to Chichen Itza and stand in front of the Tenth Century Temple of Kukulkan, they think they were looking at a Book of Mormon temple."

"Others have labeled nothing as Book of Mormon. Both approaches are wrong," Dr. Bingham added. "Most post Book of Mormon sites have been proven to be built on cities from Preclassic Book of Mormon times. The best examples of these are Copan, Palenque, and Uxmal—all post-Book of Mormon at least in their visible structures."

"How should they be analyzed," Amy asked.

"The best approach is to analyze the civilization that existed during the time the Book of Mormon history was written. We can then develop a better understanding of the Book of Mormon and the people whose lives graced the pages of the book. The most practical place to begin is the Maya region, primarily because this is where the written language evolved on the American continent—during the time of the Book of Mormon."

"Didn't other people use written language during this time?" Sal asked.

"Not to our knowledge," Dr. Bingham responded. "Even the Inca of Peru, who developed an advanced civilization during post Book of Mormon times, were illiterate."

The flight attendant's voice came over the intercom, interrupting the discussion. She said quickly in Spanish, then in heavily-accented English: "Ladies and gentlemen. We are now preparing to land. Please return to your seats. Put your seat and tray table into a full upright position."

The plane swooped over the thick, dense jungle, finally landing in a grassy clearing. The 'fasten seat belt' sign went off. Brother Moody stood. "Please remain in your seats for one moment," he said. "I wish we had two days to tour Tikal. The ruins are so extensive it would take that long to do it justice. However, because of time limitations we had to plan on just one day. Write down any questions you have and we will attempt to answer them tonight after dinner. A bus from the Jungle Lodge will take us to Tikal. Lunch will be at the Jungle Lodge at 12:30."

"We'll divide into two groups," Dr. Bingham said, "One with Brother Moody and one led by me. Note the engineering skill of the Maya, but also look around at the jungle splendors. Tikal is a national park, one of the few accessible areas of the Peten that has not been taken over by agriculture. Native flora and fauna still flourish relatively undisturbed here."

Sal and Amy stayed close to Brother Moody. The heat of the sun had not been exaggerated; jungle heat hung heavily on the passengers. During the twenty-minute bus ride Brother Moody pointed out various trees—ceiba, palm, chicozapote, and cedar—that abounded in the jungle. Monkeys roamed among the treetops and hundreds of birds flew overhead. Before they got off the bus he handed each of them a small bottle of water. "It's easy to get dehydrated."

They hurried to keep up with the tour group. Brother Moody stopped before a massive temple. "This is the Temple of the Giant Jaguar," he said. "It stands over the vaulted tomb of Double-Comb—one of Tikal's greatest rulers. This entire area," he swept his arm in a semi-circle, "is known as the Great Plaza. By the time of Christ, the Great Plaza had already taken its basic form, with platforms and stairways constructed on the north side. Over the next few hundred years, the city grew in extent and height, as old buildings were razed and covered over with new ones, and tombs set into the plaza floor.

"The corbeled arch came into use during this period, as did new-style three-colored pottery vessels. Trading was common. The people of Tikal traded for jade, obsidian, and other useful raw materials from people all over Mesoamerica.

"The Classic era of Tikal ..." Brother Moody's voice droned on, but Sal's turned on his imagination. In his mind's eye, he saw the thousands of people who built temples to ever greater heights, dammed ravines to form reservoirs for seasonal rains, and constructed causeways connecting different parts of the city and providing trade routes to other Mayan centers.

Brother Moody continued. "To correlate with the Book of Mormon the North Acropolis of Tikal was constructed about 600 BC. During the Preclassic era the people dug huge defensive trenches to protect the city—similar to what Captain Moroni describes in the Book of Alma."

"Can we see them?" Bill asked.

"No," Brother Moody replied. "The Tikal earthworks are north of here and there is really not much to see."

"Tell us about them," Bill said.

"There really is little to tell. Archaeologists discovered them in 1967. The earthworks extend across the front of Tikal for about 10 kilometers—probably built to include the huts of workers and farmers. The trench was four meters wide, with a vertical depth of three meters. It has a continuous raised embankment along the south side and passes up and over hills, all in a straight line. Several causeways or gates cross it to give passage to the defenders. Impassable swamps on both the east and west ends of the trench helped to make a pretty effective defensive barrier."

Sal wanted to move on to the temples that rose up like huge teeth out of the open mouth of the jungle.

"There seems to be similarities between some of this architecture and that of Teotihuacan," John commented.

"Yes, there is evidence of extensive trade between the two cities—especially in post-Book of Mormon times."

"How did they build so much?" Amy asked.

"Probably with slave labor," Brother Moody responded. "During the Classical Era, the Maya priests ruled totally. They controlled the social, religious, and commercial activities of the people."

"Did the people live in these temples?" a lady asked.

"Some priests or rulers may have lived in the complex, though most archaeologists feel the temples and palaces were used solely for religious purposes. The common people lived in a circular city surrounding the temple complex. Thousands of foundations of houses of stone and wood have been found. At least 50,000 people lived in and around Tikal—perhaps many more. The most visible evidence of a large population, a bountiful agriculture, and a highly-developed social organization, is the very magnitude of Tikal itself."

"What do you mean?"

"Building the city required the labor of many workers over long years to carry the rock and rubble needed to fill the bases of temples. Masons built retaining walls, and later faced structures with carefully cut blocks. Limestone was burned to make lime for mortar, a process that required the cutting of immense quantities of wood. All this had to be done with brute human labor.

"While all this labor was going on, artisans carved low-relief sculptures of stelae, and incised designs into beams of chicozapote. This wood, carved when fresh and soft, becomes iron hard when exposed to air. When you look at the temple lintels, the finest examples of Mayan wood carving, note how they have endured the jungle climate for centuries.

"Additional workers had to patch up fallen bits of plaster, replace missing blocks of limestone, keep the temples painted, plaster over floors worn with use, and maintain the reservoirs. Artisans created jewelry and beautiful pottery vessels with painted scenes of daily life, and jade jewelry and mosaics of shells and tones for personal decoration and as funerary offerings. Priests had to preside. Ball players played ball.

"Few of these workers could have devoted much time to growing food, so in addition to the workers and nobility of the city, there must have existed a large class of farmers. The Maya of Tikal took seemingly dreadful jungle swamps, with their store of water, and reworked them into resources that supported large population centers. They dug drainage canals and piled up earth to create raised planting beds where they farmed cassava, yams, corn and ramon nuts." He took a deep breath. "And in addition to all of those people, there was a standing army to maintain, and workers needed to build a defensive complex to protect the city." It was the longest lecture he had given.

After lunch, Sal and Amy wandered around the complex. The very vastness of Tikal was awe-inspiring. They went into the temples and climbed the pyramids. After a long climb, they sat down on the very top of a large pyramid. From their observation site they could gaze at the Great Plaza and roof combs rising up from the sea of jungle. "Can you imagine," Amy said dreamily, "when thousands of people dressed in colorful clothing moved around in the squares below."

Sal nodded. "And stretching beyond the city cultivated fields dotted with houses." They sat, enthralled with their imaginations until Sal noted the time.

"We have to go if we are going to catch the bus back to the airstrip." He sighed. "It's almost too wonderful to be real."

During the plane trip back to Guatemala City, Sal's mind dwelt on what he had seen. He wished he had several more days to explore Tikal. There was so much to see. So much to learn. So many questions left unanswered.

Chapter 10

The morning was absolutely gorgeous! Sal yawned and stretched. What a contrast to the tropical heat of the last few days. What did the local Chamber of Commerce call Guatemala? *Land of eternal spring.* He could believe it. He sat up on the edge of the bed. *What is scheduled for today?* As he pulled on his shoes he looked at the agenda. Saturday, June 27. *Early morning temple session for those desiring it. Morning lecture. Breakfast at the hotel. Check out.* A knock interrupted his thoughts. "Who is it?"

"Amy. Are you ready?

"Ready for what?"

"For the temple, silly."

"We can't go to the temple." "We can walk around it. Hurry or we'll miss the bus."

Sal smiled as he dressed. *Maybe someday I'll take her to the temple for real.* The thought surprised him. *Well, why not?* he asked himself. Then he remembered why not. *I'm a transplanted Mexican. I'm not a Mormon, and I'm really not good enough.* He ground his teeth in despair.

The temple, set in a splendor of flowers and trees raised its white spire regally into the azure blue sky, drawing his eyes upward. Amy pulled him down on a bench near the flower beds and they sat in silence, absorbing the sight. In the visitors' center they looked at the murals depicting life among the early Nephites—supposedly in this valley. Artist's renditions of Mayan ruins lined the walls. Amy dragged Sal into the small theater where they watched "Man's Search for Happiness." Sal had seen the film before with Amy, but thrilled to hear it in Spanish. Tears ran from his eyes as he contemplated God's plan for him. *Marriage, children—an eternal family? Could it be?*

In the morning lecture, Brother Moody talked about Alma, Abinadi, and King Noah. He stressed the significance that "one man, Alma, listened to Abinadi, and because of that one man many generations of Nephites were affected." Brother Moody traced Alma's lineage down through Alma the younger, Helaman, and his son, Helaman, Nephi and Lehi, and finally the Nephi that was on the earth at the time the Savior appeared to the Nephites.

"I would guess that the fourth Nephi, and Mormon and Moroni also came through that lineage," Brother Moody said. "Thus, God was able to call every major prophet from Alma to the closing of the Book of Mormon, just because Alma listened." He looked around the room. Tears glistened in the professor's eyes. "Not only that, but each of us is here because Alma listened. Never underestimate the power of one committed person."

Dr. Bingham started talking but Sal still attempted to digest Brother Moody's comment. *The significance of one man. The power of one committed person. He thought of his own quest for truth. Am I committed? Or just curious?* He shook his head. Amy nudged him and he refocused on Dr. Bingham.

"Today," he said, "we will visit Lake Atitlan. Many Mormon archaeologists believe it is the 'Waters of Mormon' spoken of in the Book of Mormon. During the bus ride, you may want to read about Alma and the Waters of Mormon. Think about their significance." During much of the four-hour bus ride to Lake Atitlan, Sal dozed, his head resting on Amy's shoulder. He woke when the bus came to a sudden stop. Out the window stood green-uniformed soldiers, sub-machine guns hanging casually on shoulders. They surrounded the bus. He tensed, but no one else seemed nervous. Two soldiers boarded the bus, asking to see everyone's passport.

"Seems like harassment," Sal grumbled.

Brother Moody heard him. "There is a reason for it. Guatemala has suffered through almost twenty years of civil unrest. Rebels hide in the hills and come out occasionally to raid the people. These government patrols at least keep the roads open and fairly safe."

The bus started again and then pulled into a view area. Sal watched as the files of uniformed soldiers marched down both sides of the road into the distance. Far below them he saw the lake— Lake Atitlan. Awesome! The lake, surrounded by mountains, shimmered in the bottom formed by their convergence. On the south, two huge, cone-shaped volcanoes spewed tendrils of smoke into the afternoon sky.

"We'll have little time to explore the lake today." Dr. Bingham said. "Check into the hotel and allow yourself some time for shopping and sight-seeing. The Indios here are a pure strain of Mayan and probably look much like the Mayan people did. Many little roadside shops have fantastic handmade woven cloth." He smiled, "Perhaps the 'fine-twined linen' the Book of Mormon speaks of."

Sal and Amy checked into the Hotel Del Lago—"Hotel of the Lake"—then wandered around the small lakeshore town. Dr. Bingham was right. Vendors along the roadway displayed beautiful multi-colored tapestries. Sal, though limited on funds, bought a tablecloth for his mother.

After a pleasant, evening boat ride around the lake, Brother Moody gave his evening lecture. "The Waters of Mormon give insight into the ordinances of the early Nephite Church," he said. "Here, we suppose, Alma escaped with several hundred converts. He baptized them and taught them about the baptismal covenant. This rugged area formed a refuge for this small Christian community until spies from King Noah discovered them. When told about the approach of King Noah's army, Alma took his people into the wilderness, heading north towards Zarahemla."

The next day was Sunday. Following a morning worship service, the tour group went on another boat ride. This time it was just across the lake to the village of Santiago Atitlan. "This village is our prime candidate for the Book of Mormon city of Jerusalem," Dr. Bingham said. "Remember that upon entering the borders of the Lamanites, the sons of Mosiah separated themselves and went to different sections of the land. Aaron, one of the Sons of Mosiah, went to the city of Jerusalem. We know little about that city except it was near the forest of Mormon and was covered with water at the time of Christ's crucifixion."

"Why this particular village?" Ralph asked.

Dr. Bingham answered, "The site must meet several criteria: First, it must be located near the borders of the Lamanites and near the borders of the Land of Mormon; Second, it must be on an inland lake not too far from the City of Nephi, and I might say, Lake Atitlan is about ninety miles from Guatemala City; Third, there must be evidence that the city was settled dating to 100 B.C.; lastly, there must be geological evidence of water covering the area. Santiago Atitlan meets all of those qualifications."

"Did the lake just rise and cover the village?" Sal asked.

"No. Evidence from about the time of the Savior's crucifixion indicates the volcano of San Pedro erupted, causing water to cover the city."

Check out from the hotel was routine, and soon they were on the bus again. The climb up from the lake strained bus engines, but finally they topped out. Three hours later, after traveling through the highlands, they pulled into the city of Quetzaltenango. Lunch was at La Finca and in the afternoon they had a tour of the village of Almolonga.

"This may be the land of Helam spoken of in the Book of Mormon" Dr. Bingham said. "Remember that when Alma took his people and departed from the Waters of Mormon, he journeyed towards Zarahemla. Mormon records that the Land of Helam was a very beautiful and pleasant land and that it was a land of pure water." He motioned him with his arms.

Amy had already been taken in with the beauty. The bus had toiled up the hills to a summit of 10,000 feet and the scenery from both sides of the road was awesome. She took Sal's hand and snuggled against him. "This is wonderful. I'm so glad you talked me into coming."

Sal, enjoying the snuggling. He didn't remind her Brother Moody had talked her into coming.

Dr. Bingham was talking. "Almolonga is about eight days journey on foot from the Waters of Mormon, and then is one more day's journey to the Valley of Quetzaltenango, which I propose is the Valley of Alma. From here, it is a twelve day journey on foot to Comitan, Mexico, through the rugged Sierra de las Minas mountain gap, making a total of twenty-one days of walking from the Waters of Mormon to Zarahemla. That fits the time the Book of Mormon says Alma and his people took to make the journey. The direction, time, elevation, and natural boundaries all fit."

The next day blurred in Sal's mind—more interesting ruins and quaint Indian villages.

"This is the area," Dr. Bingham said as they stood in Huehuetenango at the archaeological site of Zaculeu, "where we feel the battle described in Alma 16 took place. Notice the ruins of the post-classic city along a river. This is the headwaters of the Grijalva River, which we feel is the best candidate for the River Sidon."

As the bus ground to a stop at the Mexican border, Brother Moody said, "We'll soon cross the Grijalva River.

Near here," he said, "are the ruins called La Libertad, a candidate for the City of Manti."

Sal shook his head. *They know each area so well and tie it to the book.* He dozed as the bus quickly dropped in elevation into the Chiapas Depression. Amy nudged him awake. Brother Moody was talking.

"The evidence is not conclusive, but the geography, when tied to archaeological history, indicates this area to be the Land of Zarahemla."

"Will we see Zarahemla's ruins?" Sister Hull asked.

"I wish we could," Dr. Bingham said. "A few miles west of us are the ruins of Santa Rosa, which we believe was Zarahemla, but they are presently buried under the waters of a reservoir."

That made Sal sit up in his seat, his argumentative soul aroused. "I'm curious," he said sourly, "If the ruins are covered with water, how can you identify them?"

Dr. Bingham looked a little sad. "Before the dam was built, our archaeologists spent much time in the ruins. The site was explored enough for them to hypothesize that it could have been the ruins of Zarahemla."

Bus engines ground into lower gears as they climbed out of the Chiapas depression. Soon they were in pine trees. It was almost as if he were back in the mountains of New Mexico. "The area we are going through," Dr. Bingham was saying, "may have been the Land of Gideon, which you remember was east of Zarahemla. Tonight we stay in the town of San Cristobal de las Casas."

The journey seemed to take forever, but after driving through the low valley of Chiapas, San Cristobal was a pleasant surprise. The village sat in a high valley, and the temperature seemed twenty degrees cooler—like being back in the highlands of Guatemala.

Sal, Brother Moody, and half the tour group checked into the Hotel Bonampak. He was upset when Amy went with Dr. Bingham and the rest of the group to the Hotel Parador Cuidad Real. Dinner was served in each hotel, making the first meal he had been separated from Amy since they left Mexico City. He didn't understand how to use the telephone, which frustrated him greatly. He was sullen during dinner.

The evening lecture was in the Hotel Parador. As they loaded on the bus for the short trip, Brother Moody tried to feel him out. "Well, Sal, you've seen a lot of country, much of it related to the Book of Mormon times. What is your impression?"

Sal's sour mood showed in his answer. "Seems there's still a lot of guessing in trying to match up the ruins with the Book of Mormon."

The first stop in the morning, after getting the group together, was the offices of the New World Archaeological Foundation. A Brother Lowe greeted the group and gave them a short tour through the office complex. "This is where scholars stay when they come from BYU," he said. "We house them and help them with their studies."

Sal noticed room after room of stored sacks filled with dirt. At one table a Hispanic, who looked very Indian, sorted a sack of dirt.

"What are you doing?" Sal asked him in Spanish. The worker showed him small sea shells, bird bones, and other things he had separated from the rubble. "Finding anything that doesn't seem natural," he said.

Sal thought about the exacting work the man was doing, and wondered again if he wanted to be an archaeologist.

The Chumula Indian Village was interesting. Amy bought several brightly-colored shawls for her mother. Sal didn't spend any money, but marveled at how anyone could live in such ramshackle shacks, open at each end as they were. Inside firepits smoked up the house. The roof had openings on each end, permitting smoke to exit one side or the other, depending upon which way the wind blew. Sides of the shacks were most often mud and wattle—straight sticks stuck upright in the ground and daubed with mud—or sheets of rusted tin. Streets or sidewalks did not exist.

Chiapa de Corzo was their next stop. Dr. Bingham showed them the reconstruction of one small temple right by the road. A few blocks away were reconstructions of two more temples, with untouched mounds extending in all directions. "This was an extensive ceremonial center," Dr. Bingham said. "Most tourists only see the small temple by the highway, but these mounds have been explored extensively by Foundation archaeologists since the mid-fifties. In fact, the father of Brother Lowe whom you met yesterday was the prime archaeologist on this project. His conclusions helped other archaeologists to come up with the supposition that this was possibly the Nephite city of Sidom."

"We have one more treat this morning," Brother Moody said. "While here, we will take a boat ride on the Grijalva, into the spectacular Sumidero Canyon. The Grijalva probably carried the boats of Captain Moroni and his soldiers as they traveled back and forth from Bountiful to Zarahemla."

"What does Sumidero mean?" Sister Hull asked.

"An Indian word. The Indians of the area tried to escape the Spanish conquistadors. Rather than be captured, many leaped to their deaths from the high cliffs overlooking the canyon."

The river trip was all Sal hoped for. Motor boats carried them into the canyon. Black cliffs rose to awesome heights. The slow-moving river gave plenty of opportunity for taking pictures. Sal tried to picture in his mind what it would have been like in Nephite times, with crude log canoes rowed by warriors in loinskins. He said nothing as they rode from Chiapa de Corzo to Tuxtla Gutierrez. He wrote notes on the beauty of the canyon and the special feeling he had as he boated on the river that was perhaps the Sidon in the Book of Mormon.

In Tuxtla they stopped at the Flamboyant Hotel, Brother Moody announced, "You have the rest of the afternoon to rest or whatever. By the way," he winked at one of the ladies in the front seat, "there is a new shopping center in Tuxtla—an enclosed mall."

"I hope you don't want to go shopping," Sal said.

"No," Amy replied. "Dr. Bingham told us there's a fabulous museum here. I'd rather go there." The museo disappointed Sal. The building was being remodeled and much of what they would normally see had been put in storage. There were some excellent stelae and pottery from Mayan times. They walked next door to the historical museum. Sal loved the historical objects from the time of the Spanish *conquistadores*. It was the history of his people. When they finished that museum, Sal was ready to go to the hotel and take a nap, but Amy seemed to pick up on energy. "Let's go through the botanical gardens."

Sal had been reluctant, but he became very involved as they walked down paths past multitudes of trees, vines, and plants, many identified with signs telling what they were and where they were found. A small zoo occupied one corner of the garden. A caretaker, seeing Sal's obvious disappointment at so few animals, drew him aside.

Amy listened without comprehension as the man conversed at length with Sal—with appropriate gestures and waving of the arms. "What was that all about," she asked, as they walked towards the exit.

"He said Tuxtla has a fabulous zoological park, with real-life settings." He squeezed Amy. "Of course you are too tired to go this afternoon."

"Certainly not," Amy said gamely. "If you want to go to the zoo I'll gladly accompany you."

They took a taxi. For the next three hours Sal and Amy wandered through the natural park. Toucans, parrots, lizards, big cats, snakes, tapirs, monkeys, and even crocodiles, lived in a natural habitat. Magnificent trees soared hundreds of feet into the air. Tuxtla had been hot and humid, but in the zoo, with all of its flora, the temperature seemed ten degrees cooler.

Small black, short-tailed, rabbit-like creatures roamed throughout the park—in every cage and almost underfoot. I'll bet the Nephites used these for food, he thought, then laughed. Here I have been challenging the Book of Mormon and now I'm thinking in Nephite terms.

"What are you laughing about?" Amy asked.

"Nothing," Sal said. "Something just struck my funny bone."

"Well, I was thinking," Amy said. "Can you imagine the problems Moroni and his armies must have had struggling through these thick forests?"

Chapter 11

Brother Moody coughed politely into the loud speaker on the bus. "Brothers and sisters," he began. "On your tour of Palenque, keep several things in mind. Many regard Palenque as the most beautiful and evocative of all the Mayan ruins. Palenque's buildings appear as tiny jewel casks gleaming whitely on graceful pyramids and platforms." He smiled to play down his poetic statement. "Palenque's buildings seem possessed of a unique grace and lightness."

Dr. Bingham added. "Palenque architects were true masters. Structures are lighter, giving more room inside and wider doorways. Wide overhanging eaves protected the graceful stucco bas-reliefs which decorated the facades. No other Maya area has the level of decoration of Palenque."

That seemed to be Brother Moody's clue. "Palenque is truly unique. Its rulers erected no stelae, which are usually the hallmarks of the classic Maya. Instead, its gifted sculptors carved huge panels in low relief, illustrating long texts with ritual scenes. Look for these panels in the rear interior walls of the principal buildings. Look carefully. There are more identifiable glyphs in Palenque than in all other Mayan ruins combined. In fact," he said, "some scholars believe this ruin to be the cradle of Mayan civilization."

Sal tried to sleep on the ride back to Villahermosa, but couldn't. His mind raced with the scenes at Palenque.

The ancient ruin dramatized all the professors had said, and more. He and Amy wandered through pyramids, temples and ball courts—their favorite: the Temple of Inscriptions. They had entered the temple the back way, climbing a dirt trail up through the jungle. They enjoyed their togetherness and the quiet of walking alone for a few precious moments. He had taken Amy's hand and helped her up the steep trail. In the temple, they descended damp, slippery steps to the tomb of Pacal, an ancient Mayan ruler. They studied and tried to interpret the numerous inscriptions, for which the temple was named, even observing a "tree of life" glyph in the shape of a cross, on the front of the temple.

Sal looked out the window of the bus, deeply immersed in thought. *Teotihuacan, Tenochtitlan, Monte Alban, The Tree of Life Stone in Izapa, Kaminaljuyu in Guatemala, Lake Atitlan—the Waters of Mormon, Tikal, Chiapa de Corzo, and now Palenque. Each city and each ruin added to my feelings and ground away some of my skepticism. I find myself believing now in the Book of Mormon. Everything seems so logical. Someone built these temples and these cities; someone lived and worshipped here. Why not the descendants of Lehi? Of course, others did come over the land bridge from Asia, but that doesn't detract from the Book of Mormon story.* He sighed. *And my heritage is tied up in it. Of that I am sure. I now feel pride in my ancestry instead of shame.* He looked at the sleeping Amy. *Not only am I finding out about the Book of Mormon but on this trip I am finding out about myself.* He glanced down at his olive-colored hands. *I no longer feel ashamed of my skin-color, or my heritage. By accepting the truthfulness of the Book of Mormon, I accept my lineage through Lehi . I am of the Blood of Israel. I am a Child of God. I will prove myself worthy to marry Amy.*

A lecture by Brother Moody followed dinner. "This coastal plain is probably the corridor the Lamanites followed when they came to attack Bountiful. Villahermosa is built right on the Grijalva—or the Sidon—River."

Sal thought of the deep, almost impenetrable forest he and Amy walked through at the Zoological Gardens in Tuxtla. He raised his hand. "Dr. Moody, has the coastal plain always been open country?"

"During Mayan times the region was covered with light forest." He continued, "While the Lamanites probably traveled mostly by land, my conjecture is that the Nephites probably used the Sidon/Grijalva and other rivers to move people and trade goods from Zarahemla to Bountiful and back. We suspect the cities of Moroni, Nephihah, and Lehi were all built on this coastal plain.

"Tomorrow, before we leave Villahermosa, we'll tour the outdoor La Venta museum. In it you will see some of the huge heads of the Olmec, as well as numerous stelae from various sites here in Tabasco. Then we'll travel north to the Coatzalcoalcos River near the Caribbean coast. We have never found any archaeological evidence to support my view, but I believe that's where the city of Bountiful was located."

The museum was interesting; the colossal heads awesome. Dr. Bingham pointed out how each was different: different shaped helmets, different stylized mouths, different sizes and shapes.

"They are so huge. How did they move them?" Amy asked.

"We don't know for sure, but probably they built rafts and floated them from the quarry to where they were placed."

Sal still had some questions about that. *How did they get them from the mountain to the river? Perhaps they put them on rollers and ... Suddenly he no longer thought of the museum. I only have a few more days before Amy and the tour group go back to the States.* He had tried to spend as much time with her as possible. Under Brother Moody's watchful eye, there had been little physical contact, with exception of holding hands and an occasional peck on the cheek.

The Hotel Terranova was built on the bank of the Coatzacoalcos River in Vera Cruz. The day sizzled with heat, but a cooling breeze blew across the veranda from the river. Sal took Amy by the arm. "I need to spend some time alone with you. After all, we are practically engaged."

She laughed easily, in her beautiful way. They found a porch swing and sat contentedly together watching the river. "So this might have been the Land Bountiful," Amy mused.

"I'd rather talk about us rather than Bountiful or Coatza whatever it is," grumbled Sal.

"Coatzacoalcos," Amy chided, ignoring his advances. She lapsed back into her reflective mood. "Just think. If this was Bountiful, this is where the Savior appeared after his resurrection." She looked at Sal. "Oh, Sal, I'm so glad I came." Tears glistened in her eyes. "I have so much greater appreciation for the Book of Mormon now."

"Me, too," Sal whispered, realizing now was not the time to break her quiet mood. "From all we've seen, I feel I can now honestly accept it as the word of God."

Impulsively, Amy leaned over and kissed him. "If I say it again, will you do that again?" he asked. He put his arm around her and pulled her close. She didn't resist.

The bus passed through some beautiful country after leaving Coatcalzoalcos, but Sal paid no attention. His only thought: *Amy is leaving. I won't see her for a month. I don't know if I can stand being away from her for a month.*

Sensing his mood, she whispered, "A month apart will be good for us."

He didn't answer. That comment sounded like what a well-meaning parent might say.

The crackle of the speaker interrupted his thoughts. "On the right you can see the Tuxtla Mountains," Dr. Bingham announced. "This will be where we culminate the tour. Of course, for the archaeological students, this will be their home for the next five weeks." He chuckled, good-naturedly. "We will spend the rest of the day in this area. We'll stop at the community of Santiago Tuxtla, which rests at the base of Cerro Vigia. Many scholars have become convinced Cerro Vigia is the Mesoamerican Hill Cumorah."

Mention of the Hill Cumorah caught Sal's attention. He sat up and listened.

Brother Moody took the mike. "Without a doubt, the most sensitive issue in Book of Mormon geography today is the location of the Hill Cumorah—site of the last battle and burial spot of the gold plates. Geographically, the Tuxtla Mountain area meets all the criteria for the location of that important site. In addition, the area is beautiful, with lakes, rivers and tranquility."

While he talked, Sal pulled out Palmer's book, *In Search of Cumorah*. He flipped to the eighteenth page, and reread a paragraph he had underlined: *The impact of placing Mormon's Cumorah in the State of New York is to grossly distort the geography of the Book of Mormon. Doing this makes it impossible to reconcile the internal geography of the Book of Mormon with actual maps. Without a valid geography of the Book of Mormon there cannot be any serious studies of the correlation between the geography and the Book of Mormon.*

Dr. Bingham added, "The Hill Vigia, the most likely candidate for the Hill Cumorah, dominates the terrain in this area. Tres Zapotes, an ancient Olmec site, lies on the opposite side of the hill from Santiago Tuxtla. You will have the afternoon to explore, but be back to the bus at six. While you explore, we will unload the luggage of those who will remain here for the dig."

Sal looked at Amy, then shook his head. "I will miss you," he whispered in her ear. Hand-in- hand, Sal and

Amy began their climb of Cerro Vigia. Families lived high on the hillside. Cows grazed in pastures carved out of the brush. They passed springs of water that looked so cool and refreshing that Sal was tempted to violate the rule of not drinking water except out of a bottle.

"I've been to the New York Cumorah," Amy panted. "This hill is much bigger," She stopped to catch her breath. "And much higher."

As they topped the ridge, Sal looked at his watch. Just two hours since we left the bus. Down the hill others struggled to get to the top. From their viewpoint Sal looked south at flat plains dotted with patches of jungle-type growth. Amy pulled her Book of Mormon out of her pack. "If this is the Hill Cumorah," she said in a reverent voice, "think of all that happened here." She sat on a rock, pulling Sal down beside her. Handing him the book, she said, "Please read the Sixth chapter of Mormon."

He thumbed through the book until he found the reference.

"Please read it to me," Amy said.

Sal began reading, *"And now I finish my record concerning the destruction of my people, the Nephites..."* Again the significance of Cumorah slapped his consciousness. When he read verse seven, Amy interrupted him.

"Please read that again."

He read, *"And it came to pass that my people, with their wives and their children, did now behold the armies of the Lamanites marching towards them; and with awful fear of death which fills the breasts of all the wicked, did they await to receive them."*

"Just think," she whispered. "It wasn't just the Nephite warriors who met here"—her arms swept the valley before them—"but wives and children, and grandpas and grandmas." She sighed. Tears ran down her cheeks as she contemplated the awful slaughter. "Go on," she said huskily.

"They came to battle against us, and every soul was filled with terror because of the greatness of their num-

bers. *They did fall upon my people with sword, and with bow and arrow, and ax, and with all manner of weapons of war. My men were hewn down, yea, even my ten thousand who were with me, and I fell wounded in the midst; and they passed by me that they did not put an end to my life. And when they had gone through and hewn down all my people save it were twenty and four of us, (among whom was my son Moroni) and we having survived the dead of our people, did behold on the morrow, when the Lamanites had returned unto their camps, from the top of the hill Cumorah,..."*

"Maybe they watched from right here," Amy squeezed Sal's arm.

"How many people do you think died in the battle?" Sal asked.

"Read the next verses."

He read of all those who had fallen, then mentally counted the ten thousands that were mentioned. "Counting Mormon's and Moroni's ten thousand, I get about 230,000 people." He was aghast at the number he had come up with. He went back and counted again—twenty-three, each with their ten-thousand—230,000.

Amy leaned forward, her elbows on her knees, as she gazed at the valley at the base of Vigia. "And that number probably did not include the women and children." She let that sink in, then added. "And add to that number at least an equal number of Lamanites." She sighed again. "Perhaps a million people died in this valley in that battle."

When they returned to the bus, Brother Moody visited with a small group that encircled him. "As a young man," he said, "I was taught that the Hill Cumorah was in New York. In fact," he paused and winked at Sal, "some General Authorities of the Church spoke against the idea of another Cumorah. So I left the subject alone."

"When did you change your belief about Cumorah?" Sister Hull asked quietly.

"My teaching career and studies carried me into the relationship of the Book of Mormon and Mesoamerica. I realized that for me to really understand the Book of Mormon I needed to understand the archaeological, linguistic and traditional history of the areas that were proposed as sites where Book of Mormon events took place." He sighed. "After touring these lands many times, I finally came to the personal conclusion that for me to be true to my convictions, I had to be true to the Book of Mormon. So if the Book of Mormon teaches that the Hill Cumorah is near the Narrow Neck of Land, then that's where it is."

Sal grabbed Amy's arm and drifted away from the group. "I'll get all of that in the next few weeks," he said. "Right now, what I want is to be alone with you."

Amy let him pull her into the shade of a large Ceiba tree in the center of the village. Around the trunk of the tree, villagers had laid out fresh fruits and vegetables to sell. Several benches were vacant. Sal pulled Amy down beside him and looked her in the eyes.

He felt no embarrassment or hesitation as he said, "Once before I talked to you about marriage. You told me then that you could never marry someone outside the Church, and that when you married it would only be in the temple."

She nodded.

"My birthday is next month. When I return from Mexico I want to get baptized. If I do, will you let me announce our engagement?"

Tears filled her eyes. She squeezed his hand. "Sal," she swallowed. "If we feel the same about each other then, and if you sincerely want to join the Church, then we'll make plans for marriage."

Amy's face pressed against the bus window. Sal waved until the bus was out of sight.

Chapter 12

In the States, people are celebrating Independence Day," Sal thought, *but here in Mexico it is just the "quatro de Julio," another day.* He wiped his forearm across his eyes and turned resolutely to look at the rest of the group. Six boys and three girls, plus Dr. Bingham, made up the dig crew. He would be working with these people for the next five weeks. Sal liked the serious but knowledgeable Dr. Bingham. During the tour the professor had consistently demonstrated his firm testimony of the Book of Mormon.

Sal knew a few of the others. Bill Hestler roomed with him in Mexico City and Guatemala, so he felt he knew him quite well. Bill was tall, combed his black hair straight back, and looked as Mexican as Sal. Whitt Levell was kind of a clown, telling jokes and laughing a lot. Sal wished he could be as easy-going as Whitt, whose blue eyes and blond hair were quite a contrast to his own swarthy complexion. Sal had met the others, but he didn't know them well. There was the one with the sharp face, John Brudman. He was a nervous person, always moving, never still. The tall, overweight one was named Bob. Sal had found him pleasant to be around. Bob had been on a mission to Argentina and spoke excellent Spanish. The fellow Sal knew least about was Ralph Pearson. Ralph seemed very quiet, stayed pretty much to himself, and reminded Sal of Jim Moore who had helped him so much in Brother Moody's class. *I guess I'll get acquainted with him,* he thought. *He's going to be my bunkmate.*

The only thing he knew about the three females were their first names, Andrea, Jenny, and Betty. Betty was tall like a beanpole, brown eyes, stringy hair, and a somewhat long, plain face. She was quiet but pleasant to be around. Andrea, on the other hand, was tall, good-looking, well-built, and knew it. Andrea wore way too much makeup and acted like one of those "easy" girls. What bothered Sal was that she always seemed to have her eyes on him. He remembered when they were introduced she held his hand way too long. Sometimes at a site, she would stand next to him, her body touching his. Jenny was the most fun of the three. She lacked Betty's seriousness and the coziness of Andrea. She was open, her face filled with wisdom beyond her years. The thing Sal liked best about her was her comfortableness. She smiled all the time, seemed never down, and had a warm infectious personality.

With the orientation complete, Dr. Bingham hustled them onto a small, run-down bus. "Santiago Tuxtla does not have a hotel so we will stay in San Andres Tuxtla. It's just fourteen kilometers from here."

Sal paid no attention to the bus ride. He thought of Amy, and how lonesome she looked as her bus pulled away from the village. He swallowed as his eyes filled with tears.

The hotel was an old building, located near the edge of town on a crossroads. Years of exacting labor had gone into building fluted terraces and covered archways. White plaster patches filled in where old plaster had sloughed off. Rooms—fitted now with noisy air-conditioners—were plain but comfortable. Marble showers and terrazzo floors accented the Spanish motif. Small huts with roofs woven from palm branches provided shade for the patio. Coconut trees, loaded with deep green to ripe yellow nuts, lined the driveway and parking areas.

That night, before kneeling in prayer with Whitt and Ralph, his roommates, he reread the sixth chapter of

Mormon. Again he pictured the battlefield as he and Amy had viewed it from the top of Cerro Vigia. *"His soul was rent with anguish."* Sal tried to understand the deep, poignant feelings Mormon felt after the battle. He tried to put himself in Mormon's place: General over all the people; leading them into a battle he knew they would lose; knowing before the battle was fought that most of his people would be killed. A thought hit Sal. *Some of the people killed were his relatives. Were Mormon's wife and other sons in the battle? Did he lose brothers and sisters, nieces and nephews? Even grandchildren? Surely his children, including Moroni, had children. So grandchildren would be part of those slain! His mourning and anguish was not all just because they were his people. Some mourning was probably very personal.*

Tears sprang to Sal's eyes as he contemplated this "truth." He finally understood. Feelings were probably more important than logic. He read once more Mormon's soliloquy. *O ye fair ones, how could ye have departed from the ways of the Lord! O ye fair ones, how could ye have rejected that Jesus, who stood with open arms to receive you!* He had to stop, his eyes blurred. He had been one of those "fair ones" Mormon spoke of who had departed from the ways of the Lord and rejected Jesus. He wiped his eyes and continued reading. *Behold, if ye had not done this, ye would not have fallen. But behold, ye are fallen, and I mourn your loss. O ye fair sons and daughters, ye fathers and mothers, ye husbands and wives, ye fair ones, how is it that ye could have fallen! But behold, ye are gone, and my sorrows cannot bring your return."*

That night Sal dreamed he stood again on Cumorah. Below him, colorful armies filled the valley in a broad semi-circle. Thousands of uniformed warriors, carrying feather and cloth banners, marched against each other. The battle went on, and on, and on. He woke, wet with sweat. He thought he finally understood how Mormon must have felt.

Dr. Bingham woke them early. "Come on. There's much to do."

Sal slept until the bus ground to a halt. "Hey," Whitt said, "you and I and Ralph are a team. Let's go."

On site, one dug and sifted while the others measured, photographed, and catalogued. After the first hour, what Sal had anticipated as an exciting experience soon became tedium. Sifting through layers of dirt, looking for artifacts or evidence of any kind, did not excite him. He thought of the Indian in the Foundation warehouse in San Cristobal—painstakingly sifting through dirt for little bones and shells. He knew finding anything substantial would excite him, but all they found were a few animal bones and some broken pottery. Even that had to be examined and written down meticulously—even mapped out as to where and at what level it was found.

After a day of digging and sifting, he was ready for some exercise. The sun was still fairly high when they returned to the hotel. Thick walls in the hotel room failed to keep out the intense heat. The air conditioner did little more than create a breeze in one corner of the room. Sal sat on the edge of the bed, stripped to his underwear. He tried to read. Ralph sat at the desk, revising notes. Sal stepped into the bathroom and stripped off his underwear, standing naked in the center of the room. He looked at himself in the small mirror, then turned sideways, admiring his flat stomach. He slipped on a pair of jogging shorts and stepped back into the room. Flopping on the bed, he tugged on his Saucony running shoes. "I'm going to get some exercise," he said.

Ralph turned and peeled off his glasses. "You ought to wear a shirt. You might get sunstroke." "Naa," Sal replied. "I'm used to the heat."

He walked across the patio, past the coconut palms. He stretched, ending with some deep bends. Back on the patio, an easy lope took him across the parking apron and out the old-broken white gate. The highway was narrow, two lanes with no shoulder. Tall grass grew right to the blacktop.

Within a hundred yards he knew he should have listened to Ralph. The sun beat unmercifully upon his bare back, the heat of the day stifling. "Just my luck to get sunstroke," he murmured. "It would have been better to run in the morning or evening," he grunted in cadence with his breathing. "Too late now, I'll get at least half-an-hour in." He began counting his steps, setting a brisk, mile-eating pace, aware of the heat and its toll. He saw visions of Amy in the shimmering heat waves rising from the pavement and wondered if he were hallucinating.

Heavy, canvas-covered trucks passed on both sides of the narrow highway. One truck forced him out into the tall grass as it rolled by, its' rear wheels at the edge of the blacktop. He ran easily, even in the heat. His body, in excellent condition, responded well. Aware of the heat and its effect, though, Sal slowed to a walk after the first mile, letting his breathing slow. His skin burned and he knew he was burning, but he kept on. Three miles down the road he knew he had to get some shade and cool off. A little town, lay lazily beside the road. On the hill dead ahead—up a long flight of stairs—stood an old church, its leaning cross stark against the blue sky.

He walked up the stairs, too hot and tired to jog. The steps reminded him of those of the pyramids he had climbed in the last few weeks, except longer and flatter. Fifty-two steps— symbolically like the Mayans. His body now felt the heat more than ever. Grass grew in multitudinous cracks in the rock steps, as if they were rarely used.

His thoughts returned to some of the ruins they had visited; with thoughts of how quickly man's creations returned to nature in this tropical climate. A few more years and the steps would be so overgrown no one would know they were even there.

The church itself was old. Like the steps, years of neglect had left it run-down. Palm fronds, tied in bundles, arched over the opening where a front door had once hung. Inside there was not the coolness Sal sought but at least it was shade. Walls were green with mold from years of intruding rain. Part of the roof was missing, as was the panel above the door, making a convenient place for birds to fly into the shade of the chapel. Their evidence was everywhere, droppings all over the old concrete floor. Sal watched where he stepped.

The front wall was dominated by a large, faded, and cracked picture of the Virgin Mary, framed with more palm fronds. On each side, smaller pictures of an agonized and emaciated Christ stared out at the empty church from beneath his crown of cruel thorns. Sal's upbringing in the Catholic Church all came back to him. Unconsciously, he genuflected, making the sign of the cross on his bare chest, then stood, embarrassed.

Against the wall, on the shelf under the picture of the virgin, small glasses and vases, blackened by candles which once burned within them, stood in random order. Sea shells lay in wild abandon among the glasses, as if put there as offerings to the maid of Nazareth. Sal walked to the altar—a humble altar, inside a humble church—an old box, covered with a white cloth. Centered on the altar squatted an old pottery bowl. He looked at it. Coins of various denominations filled the bowl to the brim.

"As poor as these people are," he said aloud, "and as run down as this old church is, they still give their offerings. They still seek the blessings." He shook his head in amazement. He stood there confused, stirring of his own religious upbringing and his mother's humble faith tugging at his emotions.

In contrast to the bird-droppings on the floor, the pews were clean—as if someone had wiped them off. He sat down and thought of the people of the almost-deserted village who weekly must trudge up the steps to worship in this dilapidated church. *"What makes people hold* onto their religious beliefs? What is there about man that he has to have a belief in some supreme being— some force beyond himself?" He had asked the same questions as he stood on the Pyramid of the Sun in Teotihuacan and near the ruins of the seven-tiered Templo Mejor in the center of Mexico City. But this seemed different. There, in those grand pyramids and temples, the priests had promulgated religion. The people were but pawns controlled by their superstitions. Here, the priests had deserted their flock and left the church in ruin, yet the people still worshipped. It was beyond him.

But don't I have the same longings? Didn't I desire to have some Being to worship even though I felt I had rejected my own Church? Isn't my concentration on the Book of Mormon actually a desire within myself to find that Being, rather than just to satisfy Amy? He shook his head then knelt on the bar of the last pew—looking at the tortured, emaciated face of the Savior. "Father-in-Heaven, I no longer believe in the kind of God pictured here, but I do believe in your Son who died on the cross. Help me to find my own heritage. Help me to have pride in myself and my people. Help me to know where I came from and why I am here on this earth." He paused and looked at the icon of Mary. "And help me to understand the role of that perfect woman who became the mother of your Son." He mumbled some other words and closed his prayer, still looking at the pictures before him.

Silence was intense. Not even a buzz of insects broke the stillness of the old church. The sanctuary even seemed to deaden the roar of the trucks on the road below. A warmth, not caused by the heat of the day, filled his heart. It was as if a whisper came to him, *"Salvador Hernandez, you are doing my will. Be faithful."*

Back on the road, he glanced back once more at the little ruined church on the hill. "I am beginning to understand." he said aloud.

After a few hundred meters a trail left the road, bordering a small lake. He followed it and jogged along the gray-white sand. It seemed cooler along the water than on the highway and he enjoyed seeing the multitude of shells scattered in the sand. He came to a small fishing village. Men sat in boats repairing nets. One villager carefully painted a name on the prow of a small boat.

"Buenos tardes," Sal called as he passed.

"'Nas tardes," came the cheerful reply.

Sal stopped in the shade of a coconut palm and looked over the scene. Out from the village, small boats in disarray clung tenaciously to anchor ropes drooping into the water. Pelicans sat along the gunwales of several, filling entire boats with their alert bodies. Occasionally one would fly out, flapping occasionally as it skimmed across the surface of the water looking for food.

Back at the hotel he quickly showered, slipped on his swimming suit and stepped to the edge of the pool. His dive cleanly cut the tepid water. He swam easily across the pool, did an underwater turn and breast-stroked back across the pool below the surface. The exercise felt good. The water was cool after being in the hot sun. He relaxed, taking slow and lazy strokes through the water. His reverie was interrupted by laughter as some of the other dig members approached. He could hear Andrea's low-pitched giggle and Bob's booming laugh.

"Hi, there you are," Bob cried when he spotted Sal. "Dr. Bingham wants us to be to his room at 9 PM."

Sal pulled himself out of the pool, aware of Andrea's amused smile. He grabbed a towel and started for his room. "I'll be there," he called over his shoulder.

Dr. Bingham led the discussion. "It's important for you to have a knowledge base for either believing or discounting Cerro Vigia as the Mesoamerica Cumorah," were his opening remarks. "Today we barely got started on what I believe is a promising dig. We hope in the next weeks to find some evidence that Cerro Vigia fits the necessary criteria to be the Mesoamerica Hill Cumorah."

"What are those criteria?" Sal asked, fanning himself with his notebook.

"Several things must conform to what we know from the Book of Mormon as far as location," Dr. Bingham said, illustrating points on the blackboard as he talked. "First, we know the Hill Shim from which Mormon moved the plates was near Cumorah. Second, we know the narrow neck of land separated the Land Southward from the Land Northward. Third, we know the City of Desolation was in the Land Northward and was near the Narrow Pass that led into the Land Southward."

"Has anyone identified the narrow pass?" Jenny interrupted.

"If you were driving from the City of Tehuantepec toward Acayucan," Dr. Bingham said, "you would notice the flat plains along Tehuantepec suddenly devolve into a very narrow passageway for a distance of several miles. You would be hemmed in by mountains on either side. This route is a natural corridor between the Land Northward and the Land Southward. My conclusion is that this is the 'narrow pass' spoken of." He spread his hands and looked around. "Of course there are other possibilities. Where was I?"

"You'd mentioned three of the criteria for locating the Hill Cumorah," Ralph said, his pen poised above his note pad.

"Right. The fourth criterion is that the Hill Shim was close to the City of Desolation. Therefore, we can conclude that the narrow Neck of Land is close to the Hill Cumorah, perhaps a distance less than fifty miles."

"What about the waters of Ripliancum?" Ralph asked. "I thought they had to be close to Cumorah."

"Some who expound the one Cumorah theory suppose that the Great Lakes are the Waters of Ripliancum."

"But that's not what you believe," John said. He stood up and nervously paced behind the group.

"You're right. I cannot subscribe to that theory. There is a water basin just north of Vigia called the Papaloapan Water Basin. It is an excellent candidate for the Waters of Ripliancum. Also, there are many lagoons of water near Villahermosa."

"What if the One Cumorah people are right," Ralph asked, "and the only Cumorah is the New York Cumorah?"

"A good question." He pointed at each of his diagrams as he talked. "If the Hill Cumorah where the last battles took place is in New York, then the Narrow Neck of Land and the narrow pass need to be in the United States. If the Narrow Neck of Land and the narrow pass are in the United States, then the Land of Zarahemla and the Land of Nephi have to be in the United States. If the Jaredites, Nephites and Lamanites lived in the United States, then a massive parallel civilization existed in Mesoamerica at the same time."

"Is that possible?" Ralph pressed.

"The possibility always exists, but there is virtually no evidence that a massive civilization existed in the New York area during the time the Book of Mormon history took place. Nor was a written language in use around the New York area during that time."

"So this is the only Cumorah," Andrea giggled.

Dr. Bingham took off his glasses and polished them. "I don't want to confuse you," he said. "I sincerely believe Cerro Vigia is the archaeological Cumorah, but please don't let anything I have said lessen the importance or the sacredness of the Hill Cumorah in New York. That hill, where Joseph received the plates from Moroni, will always be Cumorah for the general membership of the Church. Moroni had to move the plates from Mesoamerica to the unnamed hill in upstate New York, because the only place the Gospel could have been restored and where the gold plates could have been translated and published in the early 1800's, is the United States of America."

Chapter 13

Buried ruins of Tres Zapotes, seemingly endless mounds, lay in widening patterns around the base of Cerro Vigia. Sal shifted his gaze to the broad valley of Cumorah. The valley, blessed with rich volcanic soil and abundant rainfall, seemed exceedingly fertile. *It is a land,* he thought, *which could adequately supply the food needed by Mormon's people. And since this is country Mormon knew well, perhaps he felt an advantage over the Lamanites in the coming battle.*

From where Sal sat on top of the mountain, the dig looked small and inconsequential. People were so small he couldn't even make them out. He hoped Whitt and Ralph and the dig crew were getting along all right without him. Leaving in the middle of the day had been wrong, but he needed to get away. What more likely place to get his thoughts together than the top of Vigia. *So far we haven't found a thing to link this mountain to Mormon's Cumorah, and yet I feel it must be so.* He looked around and then laughed aloud. *I, the great doubter, the skeptic, with no hard evidence whatsoever, accept this mountain as Cumorah.* He picked up a small volcanic stone and threw it down the hillside, the sound of its falling absorbed by the greenery. A rabbit, startled by the falling rock, darted from the bush and ran across a clearing below him.

Sheep-like cumulus clouds gamboled across the blueness of the sky. *What a beautiful day. If only Amy could be here to enjoy it with me.* He sighed aloud and looked inland at the expansive plain. Northward the sun glimmered from numerous ponds—the Papaloapan lagoon system. Dr. Bingham had taken the dig crew to the lagoon system and into a tangle of rivers and swamps known as "La Mixtequilla." These, he had pointed out, were probably the waters of Ripliancum. He also pointed out that Mormon talked about "fountains" of waters at Cumorah. Sal had witnessed these for himself, water sprang from the hill and ran down its sides in small streams.

Hating to leave, but knowing he must, Sal made his way back to the dig. The crew had finished their siesta and returned to work. No one mentioned his absence, but Andrea looked up and winked. He sat down on the lip of the trench and picked up the clipboard. The preparatory work had all been done before the dig crew arrived. Trial shafts opened all quadrants of the mounds. His crew dug along one side of a trial trench. Dr. Bingham explained that because digging takes so long—reminding them that crews had been digging at Pompeii since 1748—it became necessary to sink trial shafts to see how far down the site goes, and trial trenches to determine the length and width of the site.

Every day so far had been about the same, up at 3:30 to avoid the heat of the afternoons. Work until noon, then a siesta. And work again in the late afternoon when the sun was low on the horizon. Each day was a repetition of the day before, day after day. *Patience! That's what I need is patience. Which of the Book of Mormon prophets can model that trait for me? I guess maybe Mormon himself. Patience would be required to sift through hundreds of plates in order to find those important tidbits he wanted to include in the book. Another thought hit him. Maybe God himself should be my mentor of patience. All the times the Nephites and Lamanites turned away from His teachings, and he patiently brought them back. He is the one who models patience.*

"Hey, look here," Whitt called, interrupting Sal's thoughts. The fire-blackened round of a large shard of pottery shone in the dirt. Bill carefully brushed around it. Before lifting it from the site, Sal measured and recorded the exact location of the find. Ralph carefully lifted it with his knife and Sal snapped a picture with the Polaroid.

Sal sighed. "There's more pottery on the hills around my home in New Mexico than we have found here."

"Ha!" Bill laughed.

"Sounds like the archaeologist is getting impatient." The voice was Dr. Bingham's. Sal looked around to see the kindly professor standing behind him. Dr. Bingham sat down next to Sal. "I don't blame you. There is no more painstaking job, filled with minutia, than that of an archaeologist."

Sal was astonished to hear those words from Dr. Bingham.

"In fact, I've often likened our job to that of an airline pilot. Hours of tedium and boredom, illuminated with moments of fleeting excitement. The excitement of archaeology is in the anticipation. Knowing that you may find the key, the missing piece of the jigsaw puzzle, that makes the whole thing make sense."

"That's a good illustration," Sal said. "A jigsaw puzzle with lots of pieces missing but you still have to decide what the picture is."

"Have any real finds come out of this dig," Whitt asked, leaning on his haunches.

Dr. Bingham got up, brushing the dirt from his khaki pants. "Let's discuss that tonight in the seminar."

"When was Tres Zapotes discovered?" Ralph asked.

"A good question," Dr. Bingham laughed, "and one similar to what Whitt asked me this afternoon. You probably learned in your classes that the first item on the recipe for hare soup is to 'first catch your hare.'" He laughed at his little joke. "So first, we have to have a site.

In 1860 a laborer working in a sugar cane field near here discovered something that had the appearance of an inverted iron kettle. The owner of the hacienda ordered it excavated. What they discovered was an enormous granite head, two meters in height."

"The one we saw at the Villahermosa outdoor museum," squealed Andrea.

"Right," Dr. Bingham said. "But no one even reported the discovery until Matthew Sterling's archaeological expedition to this area in 1938. In this site he discovered many ancient monuments and the famous Stela C of Tres Zapotes, now believed to give the date of 31 B.C."

"Stela C?"

Dr. Bingham smiled. "A stela found here that is in the National Museum of Anthropology in Mexico City."

"So some important finds have been discovered here?" Sal affirmed, a little surprised.

"That's right."

"In your estimation, then," Sal asked, "who built Tres Zapotes?"

The professor shook his head. "Frankly, we don't know. We suppose it was the Olmecs."

"You said earlier that you felt the Jaredites were the Olmecs." Betty joined the discussion.

"The latter part of Jaredite history is closely related to that of the Olmecs. But the finds here, especially Stela C, don't relate to the Olmecs, but to the Maya, or Nephite people." He thumbed through his Book of Mormon. "If this site really is Cumorah, then it was also the Hill Ramah of Jaredite times. Will you turn to Ether 15:11."

Sal thumbed to the reference. *The army of Coriantumr did pitch their tents by the hill Ramah; and it was that same hill where my father Mormon did hide up the records unto the Lord, which were sacred.*

"Now read on to the end of the Book of Ether and note the similarities between the Jaredites' last battle and the Nephites' last battle."

Sal read about the gathering of Coriantumr and Shiz for four years, the ensuing battles, and Ether's last words. He closed the book, waiting for Dr. Bingham to comment.

The professor waited a few more minutes to make sure everyone was through reading, then asked, "So, as a Mormon archaeologist, what would you expect to find here at Tres Zapotes?"

"Evidence of two different cultures," Bill answered.

"And two time periods," Sal said.

"Have we found them?" Dr. Bingham asked.

"Well, the Olmec head definitely comes from the earlier period," Ralph said.

"And Stela C is from the later culture," Sal added.

Dr. Bingham smiled. "So, we continue to look for additional evidence from either culture." He turned serious. "If this hill is truly Cumorah, what other criteria must it meet?"

Thinking of what he had just read, and the view he had seen just today from the top of Vigia, Sal said, "In Ether it says the army of Coriantumr camped at the waters of Ripliancum the night before their battle, so Ramah or Cumorah must be within a day's journey of those waters."

Dr. Bingham nodded.

Ralph raised his hand. "There had to be a pretty big valley—one that would hold a million people."

"Why?" Dr. Bingham prompted.

"Because that many gathered to fight the final battle."

"Good," Dr. Bingham nodded. "Others?"

Bob spoke up. "The area had to be fertile in order to grow crops to feed that size of population."

"Right."

Whitt quipped, "I'd want the hill to be high enough so that I could look down and see what was going on without the Lamanites seeing me."

"Excellent point," Dr. Bingham smiled.

"If I were wounded, and had to climb it during the night, I would hope it would not be too steep," Jennie said.

"All of these are excellent," Dr. Bingham said. "In your estimation, does Cerro Vigia meet those requirements?" "I think so," Sal said, "but don't other hills in Mesoamerica meet the requirements as well?"

"The answer is yes. Until the Lord tells us, we cannot be sure where anything took place. All we can do is look at what evidence we have and make some rough guesses. Our guess is Vigia is Cumorah for the reasons you have given and it's proximity to the Narrow Neck of Land." He added, "Let me expand on one idea. Bob said the armies of Mormon would want to gather where the ground was fertile and crops could be grown to feed such a vast number of people." He looked around. Several of the group nodded. "David Palmer said that people would only be attracted to Mormon's army if they felt they would be well fed. How does one go about feeding a million people? Fertile land nearby is one of the strongest cases for the location of Cumorah. Palmer and I both think Mormon chose to feed his people during the four year gathering period by choosing one of the most fertile areas in the Western Hemisphere."

"Is this that area?" Jennie asked.

Dr. Bingham smiled again. "Different horticulturists have said that the area of the Cerro Vigia is the most fertile area in the state of Veracruz. Two crops per year grow here. In fact, in some years they can grow three crops of corn."

"So you think Mormon selected this hill and valley for that reason?" Ralph asked.

"At least one of his reasons. No other place would have met his needs as well."

Lying in bed that night, Sal contemplated what had been discussed, and all that had transpired since leaving Provo with Amy what seemed an eternity before. The discussions, the feeling he had on the dig, his moments of contemplation on Vigia, all gave him a feeling that he could not refute: logically, the Book of Mormon must be true.

He began taking his copy of the book with him on his meandering around the hill, stopping to read, especially the chapters written by Mormon concerning Cumorah. He knelt often in prayer, asking God to give him a witness of the book's truthfulness. Day by day, on the dig, in his hot room, or on top of Vigia, his testimony grew. The physical evidence helped.

One day students in the next trench discovered remnants of weapons, obsidian sharpened into spear points and cutting edges. Not intending to hide it, but wanting something physical to touch, he secreted a small spear point in his pocket. That afternoon, on top of Vigia, he pulled out the weapon, turning it over and over in his hands, feeling the sharpness of the edges, reflecting the sun on its shiny, chipped, black surface. A crawly feeling came to him—a feeling that the spirits of those who had made this weapon, and those who had used it, surrounded him. A chill ran up his spine and he looked around. No one. But the feeling persisted, as if the spirits of those who had fought and died here remained to look over the site of their fall. He shivered again.

He remembered something he had read in freshman lit class, something from Somerset Maugham—that "the places where men have loved or suffered keep about them always some faint aroma of something that has not wholly died." Sal pulled out his Book of Mormon and turned once more to the dog-eared page where Mormon gave his eulogy. "O ye fair ones," he read. He didn't even have to look at the page to continue, he had read the passage so many times. *"O ye fair ones, how could ye have rejected that Jesus, who stood with open arms to receive you!"* He put the book down, but continued reciting aloud from memory: *"But behold, ye are gone, and the Father, yea, the Eternal Father of heaven, knoweth your state; and he doeth with you according to his justice and mercy."*

A feeling of peace came over Sal, along with a feeling that the spirits had departed. He looked over the peaceful valley without seeing it. His eyes and ears filled with the clamor and

viewed thousands of bodies lying on the valley floor, black birds—vultures and ravens—swarming down in droves to feed on the carcasses of Nephites and Lamanites. He shook himself, seeing once again the green valley and small villages before Vigia. But he couldn't shake the feeling that he had seen a vision of what had been. He thoughtfully walked down the hill to join his crew.

Chapter 14

"Can you believe it's already the middle of August?" Ralph threw a shirt into his suitcase.

Whitt yawned. "Five weeks and it seems little more than a week."

Sal disgustedly shook his head and packed his bags without response. To Ralph and Whitt the time might have gone fast, but for him the dig at Hill Vigia had seemed much longer than five weeks. Five weeks without seeing Amy. Five weeks of not being able to drink anything but bottled water. Five weeks of digging without any real success other than a few shards of pottery, some arrow and spear points, and some ancient campfire remains that included remains of bones and shells. Five weeks without even so much as a pizza. His disappointment the last week had been obvious to everyone, especially Dr. Bingham.

Bob stuck his head in the door, his smile broad and congenial. "Andrea, Betty and I thought you guys might want to come along. The shuttle bus is going to Tres Zapotes. Dr. Bingham is making his official report and saying goodbye to the villagers."

Snapping his suitcase shut, Sal straightened up. "I'm all packed. Might as well come."

As he walked to the bus, Andrea sidled up to him, her makeup heavy as usual. Her perfume was heady. Just to make conversation, Sal asked, "How is Dr. Bingham going to handle his departure?"

Andrea seemed startled by the question, as if she had expected something else. "Well," she stammered, "he has been busy the last few days making sure the inventory of objects collected has all been photographed and indexed."

"Haven't you been helping him?"

"I helped lay out the most important finds for inspection by the local government."

"Mexican laws dealing with antiquities must be pretty strict."

By this time they had reached the bus. Sal breathed a sigh of relief. He really didn't want to hurt Andrea's feelings, and appreciated her attention to him, but he was just not interested in her.

Dr. Bingham greeted Sal and Andrea as they walked up. He smiled happily. "Hi. Congratulations for being part of a very successful dig."

"Successful?" snorted Sal. "Did we really find anything worthwhile?"

Dr. Bingham seemed surprised at his outburst. "Worthwhile? Very much so. The firepits were especially important."

"How?" Sal said, feeling cynical.

Dr. Bingham smiled indulgently. "In the first place, we can carbon date the burned wood to approximate the date when the people lived here, and from the bones and shells, we can determine the main diet of the people. In addition, we found weapons and pottery which give us some idea of their habits and culture."

He laughed at Sal's chagrined look. "Sal, honestly, we found enough artifacts that I will spend the better part of this year preparing a preliminary report for the Foundation on the significant aspects of our expedition." Sal glanced at his watch as he stepped from the bus. Eleven o'clock. He looked up at the imposing mountain. There was time to make one more trip to the top. "Dr. Bingham," he said, "I'm going to climb Vigia once more. Just in case I'm a few minutes late, will you make sure my bags get on the bus?"

Dr. Bingham nodded and Sal took off, jogging up the road towards Vigia. His breath, by the time he arrived at the top, came in gasps. He opened his fanny pack and pulled out his dog-eared, paper-back copy of the Book of Mormon. He read once more of the events that had transpired here and in the valley before him: Mormon developing an army through four years of gathering; the final battle; the escape of the twenty-four survivors to the top of Cumorah; Mormon's death and the writings of Moroni.

He set the book on a rock and stood, facing first one direction, then another. As he looked into the distance, his thoughts were on the book. His eyes took in the familiar sights. *Everything I've seen and read, and the people I've talked to, all seem to indicate those events happened right here.* He looked around to make sure he was alone, then dropped heavily to his knees in the rocky soil. He took the book in his hands, bowed his head, and hesitantly began.

"Father," he said aloud, "I pray, with full faith in Thy Son, Jesus Christ, and in His holy name, that You will please bless me with the spiritual witness Moroni promised You would give about the truthfulness of this book. To this point, Father, my testimony of the Book of Mormon is based on logic and intellectual conviction. I have read it several times. I feel the Book of Mormon is all it is supposed to be; that Mormon and Moroni did live and abridge this book; that Joseph Smith did translate it through Thy power. I feel it is true, I want it to be true, my heart cries to you to witness to me that it is true."

He knelt there for some time, until the small rocks cut into his knees. He gritted his teeth and remained kneeling. "Please Father," he whispered. Opening the book to the tenth chapter of Moroni, he again read the words, *"if ye shall ask with a sincere heart, with real intent, having faith in Christ, he will manifest the truth of it unto you, by the power of the Holy Ghost."*

He sighed and started to rise to his feet. Suddenly his knees felt weak, as if they wouldn't hold up his body. He sank again to the ground, prostrating himself among the rocks and brush. A warmth—a tingling from head to toe—filled his entire body. He felt as if he were floating above the earth. No longer did he feel the pain of the rocks and sticks poking into his body—only the warmth of what seemed to him to be a feeling of total love.

Minutes passed before he gained enough strength to get to his knees. "Thank you, Father," he breathed. "Thank you for the witness of the Spirit. No longer will there be any doubt in my mind or heart concerning the Book of Mormon."

He didn't even remember the trip down the mountain; he just found himself climbing on the bus. Glancing at his watch, he was surprised to see was already 4:30, time for the bus to leave. The few minutes he felt he had spent on Vigia had actually been over three hours. The rest of the students gaily chattered as the bus drove past the site of the dig.

Sal looked back at the village of Tres Zapotes and the looming hill behind it. This little part of God's earth had come to mean very much to him. The dig had perhaps not uncovered what he thought were significant artifacts which tied the hill to Cumorah, but his being here had accomplished his primary purpose.

He didn't say a word on the way to Vera Cruz, answering others' queries with a disassociated grunt, not really even hearing their questions. His mind seemed totally absorbed by his experience. *God has spoken to me through the Spirit. God has witnessed to me that the Book of Mormon is true. God does love me, does care about me, does want me to be part of the Gospel.* He unconsciously rubbed his hands together. *I can hardly wait to share my experience with Amy.* Then he thought, *No, it was too special. I don't think I can tell anyone about it.*

The flight home was routine. Sal slept through most of it. When they landed in San Diego Sal slipped away and called Amy.

"Hello."

Her voice sent a thrill up his spine.

"Hi, Amy, this is Sal."

"Sal!"

He smiled at the excitement in her voice. "Ya. We're in San Diego on the way home. We'll get there about eight."

"I'm so anxious to see you," she said.

"Me, too." He swallowed the lump in his throat. "I love you," he whispered.

"What? I couldn't hear that last part," she said.

"That's okay. I'll tell you when I get there. Goodbye." With his finger he lowered the tab, still hanging on to the handset. He sighed, hung up the phone, then headed to the gate to catch the plane home. Andrea hailed him and some of the students tried to talk with him, but he just wanted to think. In the waiting area by the gate he chose a seat between two occupied ones waiting for the flight to be called.

On the plane, he was glad to be on the side of the aisle where there were only two seats. Bill sat next to him and neither desired to talk. Soon Sal was again asleep.

"We have been cleared to land in Salt Lake City," the flight attendant's voice on the intercom brought Sal awake. "Be sure your seat belt is fastened and your seat and tray are in the upright and locked position." Sal pushed the button, raising his seat. He glanced at his watch. Almost eight in the evening. *I wonder if Amy will be there.*

She was, and truly the proverbial sight for sore eyes as he came up the jetway. His eyes feasted upon her loveliness. She ran forward and grasped both of his hands. He wanted to take her in his arms and kiss her, but behind her he saw her serious parents and restrained himself. He wished he could have her all to himself.

"Hi, Brother and Sister Mecham," he called cheerily.

As they walked to the carousel to get his luggage, Brother Mecham put his arm around his shoulder. "Now what are your plans, son?"

Sal looked at him. He seemed sincere. Sal shrugged. "I want to get settled back in my apartment and get ready for school to start."

"You'll be going to school this semester?"

"Yes." He grunted as he pulled one of his bags from the clanking carousel.

"What will you study?"

"Advanced archaeology."

"That is a very intensive course of study."

"I know. Hey, here is Dr. Bingham." He turned to his teacher. "Dr. Bingham, do you remember Amy?"

"Yes," he smiled warmly. "How could I forget?"

Amy led him to her parents. "Mom and Dad, this is Dr. Bingham. He was one of the guides on our tour."

Other members of the dig crew came up and shook hands with them, saying goodbye as each went his or her separate way. "See ya in class!"

Sal helped Dr. Bingham pull his suitcases off the carousel, then shook his hand. "Thank you," he said sincerely. "I look forward to having a class from you this fall."

"I'm afraid that will be impossible," Dr. Bingham said. "I'll be spending my time entirely in practicums and documenting this summer's work. But I would recommend Dr. Benedict." After saying goodbye to Dr. Bingham, Sal and Brother Mecham carried the luggage to the car. He held the door for Sister Mecham to get in the front seat, and then held Amy's door for her. She smiled at him—an unspoken thank you for his politeness. He took his seat next to Amy in the back seat of the roomy Cadillac.

Amy turned to him, their knees touching. She took both his hands in hers. "I want to hear all you've done."

Sal went through the dig, condensing it down to some of the highlights. The drive to Provo seemed too short. Brother Mecham stopped the car in front of his old apartment.

"I'll be back to pick you up for supper," Amy said with a wink. "Dad feels I need to leave you alone while you get settled back into your apartment."

He unloaded the suitcases and stood on the curb as they drove away. "Goodbye," he muttered, his arm raised.

Unpacking took only a few minutes. Everything he owned was dirty. He threw the dirty clothes in the hamper, looked in the fridge, and then wandered aimlessly around the apartment. The screen door banged as someone came in. It was, Enrique, one of his roommates.

Enrique slapped him on back. "Good to see you." He grabbed a chicken leg from the fridge and munched on it. "How was your vacation?" he asked. He didn't wait for an answer but picked up his book and was soon engrossed in it.

Sal hadn't expected such a let-down. It was as if he had not even been gone. He slumped onto the couch to wait for Amy.

It was after six when Amy finally honked. Sal had roused himself enough to take a shower and change clothes.

Dinner seemed stiff and formal—especially after five weeks of cafeteria-style eating at the dig. There was little or no chance to talk about anything personal. Amy and her father seemed really interested in the dig and what they found.

"So you really didn't find anything?" Brother Mecham asked.

Sal found himself defending the dig and their finds. "Dr. Bingham seemed to think the dig was successful," he said lamely. "Especially the fire pits, pottery, and remains of weapons."

"So you found some weapons?" Amy asked. "Could they have been from the final battle?"

Sal shrugged. "Who knows?" He had a difficult time restraining himself from telling them about his experience on Vigia. But he decided that if he told anyone, it would only be Amy.

After helping to clear the table and stack the dishes, he was finally alone with her. Brother and Sister Mecham discreetly retired to the family room to watch television and Sal and Amy sat in the living room. There was a short, awkward silence while he thought of what to say. Amy turned the television on, the volume very low. He sat watching the pictures moving across the screen for a few minutes. Then, screwing up his courage, he said, "Amy, I think you know how I feel about you, and I hope you feel the same way about me. I've given a lot of thought to this over the past five weeks. And like I said before we parted in Mexico, I want to marry you."

"Oh, Sal. Shouldn't we finish our schooling first?" "I don't care when," he said doggedly. "I just want you to be my wife."

She turned away. "I told you there was a condition that I wouldn't bend on."

"That's the point," he said. "I want to marry you. And I want to marry you in the temple."

Amy didn't even look at him. He wondered if she had even heard what he said. Her eyes seemed fixed on the television. Amy wasn't seeing anything. Tears, at first just a trickle, then a flood, overflowed onto her cheeks. She turned and threw her arms around Sal's neck. It was a time when no words were necessary.

After several moments, she breathed deeply a few times to compose herself, then asked in a quiet voice. "Sal, one reason you stayed at the dig was to get a testimony of the Book of Mormon."

Still holding her tightly to him, almost afraid to let her go, Sal said, "I have a testimony, most of which came as we traveled together." The sweet smell of her hair, along with a trace of her perfume, filled his nostrils. "The dig finalized my logical testimony. Dr. Bingham helped, too." He waited what seemed like a long time before going on, but still he held her tightly to him.

"On my last day, I went again to the top of Cumorah—the place where you and I sat and talked." He swallowed noisily. "It was there the Lord fulfilled

Moroni's promise." He pushed her back so he could look into her eyes. Tears again brimmed over and ran down her cheeks. His own tears went unheeded. "Amy, I know the Book of Mormon is true. The Spirit bore witness to me."

She sighed, let go of his hand, pulled a kleenex from her skirt pocket, and wiped her eyes.

"I thought you'd be happy."

"Oh, Sal, I am. I am so happy."

He took her hands again. "Then why should we wait until we finish school to get married? Why can't we get married sooner?"

"Sal, marriage isn't something you rush into. There are things that have to be done." She sat up straighter as a thought came. "You will have to be baptized."

"I know. I've thought of that. I even wondered if your father would baptize me."

"Of course, Sal, but Church policy is that you can't go to the temple until you've been a member at least a year."

Sal's anger flared. "A year! That's too long. Let's get married first and go to the temple later."

Amy took his hand and gently pulled him down beside her. "There is a right way, Sal. And we want to have our marriage start out the right way, don't we?"

"Then I want to get baptized as soon as possible."

"Why don't we ask Dad?"

"Do we dare?"

"We'll have to ask sometime. What better time than now?" She didn't wait for his reaction, but called, "Dad! Mom!"

Sal's fear was palpable. It knotted his stomach. *How can I, a poor Hispanic, ask her rich, gringo father if I can marry her?* He mentally kicked himself.. *Wait a minute. I am a Son of God, and a descendant of the Israelites.* He straightened his shoulders.

"What is it, Amy?" Brother and Sister Mecham walked into the room and stood, waiting.

"Dad and Mom, Sal has something to ask you." Her eyes were damp but shining.

Sal swallowed, and stammered. "Brother and Sister Mecham. I-I want to marry your daughter." Out of habit he looked down at the floor. When he looked up at them, they didn't seem at all shocked. He focused on Amy's father and continued, this time without the quaver in his voice. "I want to be baptized, and Brother Mecham, I would like you to baptize me."

"This seems rather sudden," Brother Mecham said, clearing his throat. "I'll be glad to baptize you, Sal, but have you had time to really think of the consequences of marriage?"

Sal took Amy's hand and squeezed. Her return squeeze gave him courage. "I thought about it often before our trip, sir," he said, "but at the dig I thought of little else. We love each other and I believe we are ready."

"It's hard to live on love."

"Larry, give them a chance," his wife interrupted. "If they are that serious, the least we can do is start planning."

"Planning! Hah!" he said, throwing his arms into the air. "That's what you women love to do- -plan weddings." As he turned to go he smiled and winked at Sal.

Sister Mecham walked over and put her arm around her daughter. "Amy, we've taught you right from wrong and I believe you are old enough to know what is right. But this is a major decision and we do need to talk about it." She kissed her daughter on the forehead, patted Sal on his shoulder, and followed her husband from the room.

Sal didn't know what to say. He felt like jumping up and doing a dance.

Amy broke the silence. "Well, we need to set a date for you to get baptized. When will you be ready?"

It took a moment before Sal could talk. "I-I don't know. I feel as if I'm ready now."

"We'll have to contact the missionaries and find out when they are having a baptism."

Sal smiled. Amy was going to get him in front of the missionaries yet.

Chapter 15

The two young men were about his own age, Elder Bowen from Pennsylvania and Elder Hectar from California. They had a "golden" contact. Now they did not want to lose him. They started with the first missionary discussion, and proceeded to teach Sal, whether he wanted to be taught or not.

"I feel I already know what I need to," Sal said defensively, "I want to get baptized as soon as possible, so let's make it quick."

"No problem," Elder Bowen said. "We will present all of the discussions in one night."

Sal listened to them, surprised at how much he learned about God and Jesus Christ and the restoration of the Gospel.

At the chapel he met with the Zone Leader, Elder Jones, who came straight to the point. "Why do you want to join the Church of Jesus Christ of Latter-day Saints?"

Sal didn't really have to think about his answer. "I have a testimony that the Book of Mormon is true and that the Church has been restored to the earth," he replied.

Elder Jones asked many questions, some very personal, like "Are you morally clean?"

"Yes " He was glad that he could give an honest answer.

After finishing his interview, Elder Jones explained about the priesthood. "After you have been baptized and confirmed, you will have the Aaronic Priesthood—the priesthood John the Baptist had—conferred upon you."

The room was small—smaller than Sal had imagined. Several dozen folding chairs stood in a semi-circle. An accordion door on the end had been folded back, revealing the baptismal font. Brother Mecham, dressed in white, sat between him and Amy.

A man, tall, very thin, and dressed in a blue, single-breasted suit with a blue, polka-dot tie, stood up to conduct. Sal recognized him as the Bishop who had visited with him in the Ward, Bishop Sorquist or something like that. "Brothers and Sisters, this is a sacred and solemn occasion. The Mission President asked me to conduct this baptismal service."

There was an opening song and prayer, which really didn't register on Sal's mind. His mind was on other things—he wrote his mother about his baptism but had received no reply to his letter. He wondered what her reaction would be to his joining the Mormon Church; he wondered about his sisters and their teasing about how many wives he was going to have. He even thought about his father—long dead—and what he would be thinking.

The bishop said, "Jesus Christ, Himself, set the pattern for the solemn ordinance of baptism. He requested John the Baptist to baptize him in the Jordan River. Most significant for us, it was this same John the Baptist who returned as a resurrected being to give Joseph Smith and Oliver Cowdery the authority to baptize, by restoring the Aaronic Priesthood."

The Bishop continued with his testimony, but Sal's mind again wandered. He thought how he had resisted this moment—how he fought against accepting the concepts of the Church—especially the Book of Mormon. *And yet*, he thought, *the Book of Mormon converted me. I thought I would disprove it. All I did was prove to myself it was truly the word of God.*

"I testify to you," Bishop Sorquist said, "that the baptism of water which you are about to receive, and the baptism of the Holy Ghost, known as the baptism of fire, which you will receive later, will change your life, as it has changed mine." He picked up the Book of Mormon. "Nephi told us about the sacredness and purpose of baptism in Second Nephi, Chapter thirty-one." He flicked the pages.

"Here it is in verse twelve: *The voice of the Son came unto me, saying: He that is baptized in my name, to him will the Father give the Holy Ghost.* Verse fourteen talks of the seriousness of covenant you will make: *Thus came the voice of the Son unto me saying: After ye have repented of your sins, and witnessed unto the Father that ye are willing to keep my commandments, by the baptism of water, and have received the baptism of fire and of the Holy Ghost, and can speak with a new tongue, yea, even with the tongue of angels, and after this should deny me, it would have been better for you that he had not known me.*" Bishop Sorquist paused and directed his gaze at Sal.

Sal almost dropped his eyes, as he would have done in the past, but he looked into the bishop's eyes until he continued.

"Nephi goes on to say that baptism is the gate by which you enter the straight and narrow path which leads to eternal life. And then he asks in verse nineteen if all is done just because we are baptized?" Again he paused dramatically and looked at Sal. "He answers his own question. 'No,' he says, and then in verse twenty is my main message for you tonight. *Wherefore, ye must press forward with a steadfastness in Christ, having a perfect brightness of hope, and a love of God and of all men. Wherefore, if ye shall press forward, feasting upon the word of Christ, and endure to the end, behold, thus sayeth the Father: Ye shall have eternal life.*" He sighed. "That is a promise that comes to you through the waters of baptism. It is a promise not to be taken lightly."

The words kept going through Sal's head. *"Ye shall have eternal life."* He turned to look at Amy. She nodded and smiled encouragement.

Brother Mecham stood in the water. Sal walked down the steps. The water, a little cool, came about up to his waist. The moment indelibly inscribed itself in Sal's memory: Brother Mecham taking his hand in his, raising his other hand to the square, and pronouncing the words, *"Salvador Jesus Hernandez, I baptize you in the name of the Father, and of the Son, and of the Holy Ghost, amen."* He didn't feel any different when he came out of the water—just wet all over. Neither uttered a word as they left the font and went to the dressing room to change into their suits. Sal spent a little extra time to make sure his glossy hair was in place.

People visited quietly together as he came back into the room. Bishop Sorquist, who had been talking, motioned him to a chair at the front. "Salvador will now be confirmed. Will all those priesthood holders who desire to help in the confirmation please come forward."

Amy's brothers—Robert, Richard, Alan, and Bryan—all came forward. In addition, the two missionaries who had met with Sal also stood up. He looked up from his chair into the sea of their faces: eight men standing around him. Each put a hand on his head. The weight of their hands alone gave a feeling of great power—of authority.

Brother Mecham's voice filled his ears. "Salvador Jesus Hernandez, in the name of Jesus Christ, and by the power of the Holy Melchizedek priesthood which we hold, we your brethren lay our hands upon your head and confirm you a member of the Church of Jesus Christ of Latter- day Saints, and say unto you, receive the Holy Ghost."

It was as if Sal were again on top of Vigia-Cumorah. He felt the same powerlessness in his body, the same floating sensation. He had a feeling of reaching up for the ceiling, of his body being tall and looking down on everything that was happening. He pictured the eight brethren surrounding him, and himself sitting on the chair.

Brother Mecham's voice continued on with a blessing. Words and phrases came through his consciousness, "select the right mate;" "take her to the temple;" "live a life of worthiness;" "be an instrument for good in the Lord's hands." The blessing took a different emphasis. Even Brother Mecham's voice seemed to change. "Your earthly father, as well as your Father in Heaven, are pleased with the steps you have taken this day. Your father anxiously awaits the time when your mother also will enter the waters of baptism. He is anxious for his work to be done. Salvador, I promise you that if you are faithful, you will be the means of baptizing your mother and sisters, so they, along with you, can be sealed with your father in the holy temple."

Tears ran freely down his cheeks as Brother Mecham pronounced this blessing upon him.

One emotional high followed another. His ordination to the Aaronic priesthood was another spiritual experience. Everyone shook his hand and congratulated him, then the whole family celebrated by going to Baskin-Robbins for ice cream. Afterward, when he was alone with Amy, the impact of what had happened really hit him.

"Amy, I am truly a member of Christ's Church on the earth. I hold the same priesthood as John the Baptist held."

Amy didn't say anything, just squeezed his hand.

He babbled on enthusiastically. "September seventh will always be an important date in my memory book—the day I was baptized, became a member of the Church, and had the priesthood of God conferred upon me." He took her hand and turned her so he could look directly into her eyes. "Can we now set the wedding date?"

"Father said we should discuss finances and where we are going to live."

"Well, I can continue working at BYU. And I am still on scholarship."

She dropped her head. "The money you make at the receiving dock barely pays for your room and board. It wouldn't pay for an apartment."

Sal swallowed. "Maybe you can work part-time, at least for awhile?"

She seemed to ignore that comment. "Why not make this date even more special and get married next September 7?"

Sal clapped his hands in his excitement. "A wonderful idea. "I'll be ready to start my senior year and you will be a junior."

"Have you decided what you are going to do?"

"Yes," Sal said softly. "I want to be an archaeologist. I want to get my doctor's degree in archaeology so I can teach. I want to find out more about my ancestors and to work on archaeological sites of the Book of Mormon so I can help other people like me get a stronger testimony. That was a lot of talking for Sal. He looked at Amy.

She squeezed his hand again, apparently in affirmation. "That is wonderful," she breathed. "And I want to continue my education and become a kindergarten teacher. I love children and will enjoy working with them."

"Especially our own," Sal suggested quietly.

Tears again came into her eyes. "Especially our own."

"Oh, I almost forgot," Sal reached in his pocket. "This is all I could afford right now, but I promise you I will get you a beautiful diamond later." He slipped a ring on the ring finger of her left hand.

Amy looked at the CTR ring, similar to the one she had worn in Primary so many years ago. "I'm so glad you Chose the Right," she said softly.

"Being engaged and a member of the Church created many changes in me," Sal told his friend, Jim Moore over a root beer.

"Like what?" Jim asked, looking owl-eyed over the rim of his glass.

Sal shrugged and didn't speak for a moment. "I'm a better student. I'm more concerned about my grades and keeping at the books."

Jim nodded.

"And I really enjoy archaeology," Sal continued. "It is the only academic area that has really sparked my interest."

"You must have had quite the experiences this summer on the dig," Jim said.

Sal sighed. "It was a life-changing experience." He thought a moment. "But the real changes didn't come at the dig."

"Oh?"

"I visited a little run-down Catholic church on a hill. That experience made me start to question my own lack of commitment. I asked myself what made people hold onto their religious beliefs—even in the face of adversity or neglect. I asked why people needed a supreme being to worship."

"And?"

"On the hill Cerro Vigia—possibly the Mesoamerican Cumorah—I received my answer."

"Which was?"

Sal didn't answer directly. "My father died when I was a child. Though I can't see him, I feel his presence. The same thing applies to my Father in Heaven. I don't see him but I know He is there. The most important thing I learned at Cumorah was that God loves me." Jim nodded. "And that is what makes people hold to their religious beliefs?" "I believe so with all my heart."

Chapter 16

Sal had not realized one had to get up so early to get married in the temple. It was barely light. The lighted temple, shadowed by high, rock-faced mountains, stood amidst a wide expanse of lawn and flowers. It was not a strange place. Sal and Amy had come here often during the past year. Streaming in the slight morning breeze, the American flag flew proudly before the temple.

As they walked up the sidewalk between beds of multi-colored flowers, Sal took his younger sisters'—Maria Elena's and Gerda's—hands. He glanced over his shoulder. His mother, Guadalupe, with his other sister, Felicidad, trailed behind. His family had arrived on the bus from New Mexico the previous evening and Sal was excited to show them the temple.

Ahead, Amy walked between her parents, her white wedding dress draped over her arm. She turned and waved, her teeth flashing in the early morning light. Robert, Amy's oldest brother, caught up with Sal and his family. He had driven them to the temple and parked his car.

"Does your mother understand she cannot be with you during the wedding?"

Sal nodded. He knew it was difficult for his mother to understand, but she accepted it in her quiet way. Now she looked inquiringly at Sal. "After the wedding, mother, we will come outside for pictures and go to the wedding breakfast." When he mentioned the wedding breakfast, he again felt ashamed. He had discovered that the groom's family was supposed to pay for the wedding breakfast, flowers, and tuxedos. Unknowing and broke, he had let Brother Mecham take care of everything. Silently, he vowed that someday he would make enough money to pay him back.

Over the past year of his engagement to Amy, he had learned to love and respect the Mecham family—they were so close, so united, so open and accepting. From the day he announced the engagement, they had been supportive of Amy's decision, never trying to talk her out of it, never putting Sal down because he was Chicano and poor. They just pitched in and made him feel welcome and already part of the family.

Now, here they were at the temple—his wedding day, a year to the day from his baptism. It had been a long year—a year of study and frustration and desire and work—but now he was glad that they had been made to wait. He felt ready to take Amy to the temple; ready to make serious commitments and promises to Amy and God in the temple.

He offered a silent prayer as he walked into the temple foyer. *Dear God, let this be a wonderful day for Amy and me, and Father, please bless mother that she will understand and will eventually be able to come to the temple, herself.*

He made sure his mother and sisters were comfortably seated in the anteroom off the foyer, then followed Robert and Brother Mecham into the temple.

Later, as he tried to recall things, everything seemed somewhat of a blur: the temple recommend desk, the clothing, the dressing room. He was glad Brother Mecham and Robert were there to guide him. Dressed in white, sitting with half-a-dozen others who were to be married, he waited in the groom's room.

"Good morning," a tall man said brightly as he stepped into the room and closed the door. "I'm President Hall, first counselor in the temple presidency. My wife,

Sister Hall, is in talking with your brides-to-be. Let me explain to you some of what you will see and hear this morning.

"The temple endowment gives information and instruction relating to past dispensations, and emphasizes the importance of the present dispensation as the greatest era of human history. Today in the temple you will be instructed in the prominent events of the creation, the condition of Adam and Eve in the Garden of Eden, their disobedience and expulsion from that blissful abode, and their condition in the lone and dreary world. You will be instructed in the plan of redemption, the period of the great apostasy, and the restoration of the Gospel with all its ancient powers and privileges.

"You will make covenants with Heavenly Father concerning your personal purity, promising to live a life of strict virtue and chastity. You will commit yourselves to comply with Gospel requirements in your life, and to use your talents and means in spreading the Gospel. Obedience to each covenant brings a blessing, contingent upon the faithful observance of the conditions.

"I don't know what you've heard about the temple ceremony, but there is nothing in the ceremony that is not uplifting and sanctifying. In every detail the endowment ceremony contributes to morality, consecration to high ideals, devotion to truth, patriotism to nation, and allegiance to God."

He thought again of Nephi, obedient to God and developing his spirituality so he could actually converse with the Spirit. *I want to be that spiritual*, Sal thought.

In the endowment room, wearing his small pink tab which indicated a living endowment, he sat between his future father-in-law and Robert. He paid close attention, trying to relate things to what President Hall had said. Finally, the endowment was over. He sat quietly beside Amy in the Celestial Room. Someone slapped him softly on the back. He looked up. There were Ralph Pearson,

Bill Hestler, and Whitt Lavell, all friends from the dig. He jumped to his feet, gravely shook their hands, and whispered, "I'm surely glad you came."

Across the room Sal spotted Brother Moody, who waved to him. His heart was really full when Jim Moore walked up to him and took his hand. During the past year he and Jim had become very close friends. Both were enrolled in the archaeology department, and both were excited about learning more about Book of Mormon artifacts.

Though he missed having his mother with them in the temple, he couldn't have had better friends and family than those who surrounded him now. President Hall motioned to them from a doorway across the room. "He's ready for us in the sealing room," Amy whispered.

Sal nervously took Amy's hand and guided her through the throng of people. She looked so beautiful in her wedding dress. His heart felt as if it would burst, he was so filled with love and pride.

President Hall, though friendly, was very officious. While friends and relatives filed in, President Hall directed them into the proper positions, then stood in front of the altar, the wedding license in his hand. "Brother Salvador Jesus Hernandez and Sister Amy Elizabeth Mecham, this is an honor for me today to unite you young people in holy matrimony. As you are well aware, we as Latter-day Saints regard the marriage ceremony within the temple as the one and only perfect marriage contract. We recognize the legal validity of any other marriage, but civil marriages and indeed all other marriages made without the binding authority of the Holy Priesthood are contracts for this life only.

"Your temple marriage, on the other hand, holds that family relationships of earth may be made lasting and binding beyond the veil of death. Under Celestial Law, the earthly relation of husband and wife, parent and child, will endure in full force and effect, provided such relationship has been sealed on earth by the power and authority of the Holy Priesthood. Therefore, what we do in this room today will unite you, Salvador, and you, Amy, in a solemn covenant of union which shall endure beyond the grave. Your children, when they come, will automatically be children of the covenant and heirs to the Priesthood. No ordinance of adoption or sealing is required to give them place in the blessed posterity of promise."

President Hall paused and looked around the room, finally focusing again on Sal and Amy. "I want you to remember, young people, that life here on earth is just a shadow of what eternity is like. The reason people in families feel so deeply about each other is that our Father in Heaven intends that families should last forever. Our family feelings are not wiped away at death but are eternal in nature. Our loving Father puts us in family units here so we can learn and prepare to do the same thing when we return to Him. Life here on earth is a practice run on what is to come if we only prepare."

Then President Hall talked about how to make their marriage successful. Sal remembered such things as "never go to bed angry with each other," "resolve any differences before;" "pray for revelation about your marriage and then read the scriptures, because answers to your prayers will come in the scriptures;" and "pray every day together." He talked directly to Sal to "take Amy out each week on a date, even if it is just a walk, but do something just by yourselves each week." There were other things, but Sal's mind could absorb no more.

President Hall finished his counsel, smiled, and glanced down at the documents in his hand. "Salvador Jesus Hernandez, you take Sister Amy Elizabeth Mecham by the right hand ..." His voice seemed to fade as the Spirit filled Sal. It was the same feeling once again he had felt on top of Vigia-Cumorah and again at his baptism. His body felt as if it were floating above the altar. His eyes were focused on Amy, but in his mind's eye he looked down upon himself and Amy, kneeling across the altar from each other. The room was filled with people. He was surprised that there were more people than had come into the room. He saw a man whom he immediately recognized as his father, dark-haired, mustached, and smiling. He was not surprised. He had the feeling others were also relatives—grandparents he had never known. Even in that distracted state, he clearly heard each word President Hall said, even responding appropriately in the right places.

"Salvador Jesus Hernandez and Amy Elizabeth Mecham, I now pronounce you man and wife, married for time and for all eternity. Sal, you may now kiss your bride across the altar."

The view of his father's smiling face faded. He did not realize he was crying until Amy took her handkerchief and wiped his cheeks. She, too, was crying softly, her mascara running.

President Hall was talking again. "If you will both come up here, you may exchange rings, which is really not part of the wedding ceremony, but a nice custom, and then your family and friends would like to congratulate you."

Sal smiled as he pulled the CTR ring off Amy's finger. For a year it had served as the engagement ring. He had worked hard all summer at two jobs, but now was the payoff. From his pocket he pulled out a small, red-velvet box and opened the top. Two rings, studded with diamonds, were in the box. He picked them up and carefully placed them on Amy's finger. He looked up into her shining eyes.

The wedding breakfast and reception that evening were anticlimactic. Sal was glad his mother and sisters could participate and feel part of the wedding, but his mind kept returning to the sealing room and the feelings he had there. He had a clear picture of his father—a father he had never known.

"When are you returning to New Mexico?" he asked his mother. "Do the children need to be back for school?"

Maria Elena didn't give her mother a chance to answer. "Sister Mecham talked mama into staying with them this week," she said excitedly. "'Til you come back from your honeymoon."

With suitcases in the trunk, the red Grand Prix became the perfect wedding carriage. The first night the honeymooners drove no further than a hotel in Provo. They slept in, had a leisurely breakfast, then drove happily away. For six days they toured the canyons of Southern Utah, Bryce, Zion, Grand, and Cedar Breaks. They took in the Shakespearean Festival at Cedar City, Sal's first experience at seeing Shakespeare.

On their last night, he sighed contentedly as he enveloped Amy in his arms. "This has truly been a time of growing together, of uniting two souls into one, of creating goals and dreams, of making dreams come true."

"Six days are too short to fully accomplish all of that," Amy laughed.

"I know," Sal said, "but I need to be back for my job on Monday."

Maria Elena and Gerda ran to meet them as they pulled into the Mecham driveway. "You're home! You're home."

Gerda yanked open his door. "Guess what?" she screamed. "We're moving to Provo."

"Moving?" Sal hadn't thought his mother would ever leave New Mexico.

"Brother Mecham has found Mama a job at the University and we're going to live here," Maria Elena beamed.

Sal opened the door for Amy, helped her out of the car, and put an arm around each of his sisters. "So, you are going to move to Provo? What else has happened while we were gone?"

"Brother and Sister Mecham took us to Temple Square in Salt Lake City," Gerda said.

"And we heard the Tabernacle Choir," Maria Elena added.

"And we saw the statue of Jesus," Felicidad said as she came out the door, a peanut-butter and jam sandwich in her hand, and more of it smeared on her face.

Sal kissed her on her forehead and went in to see his mother. She stood at the sink, helping Sister Mecham with the dishes. There was a new light in her eyes, a new spring in her step as she gave Sal a hug.

"Thank you son," she said, her English heavily accented. "You have given me more than life." Her eyes filled with tears. "And I will once again be with your father." She put the apron up to her face and turned away, too choked up to talk.

The little apartment on 500 East, just below the University, was ready for them. They had rented it several weeks before the wedding and had taken pains to decorate it the best they could on their meager earnings. But now there were new lamps and dishes and other things from the wedding reception. They spent all afternoon putting things away—their very own things. The apartment was just right for them: a small kitchen with a table that would only seat two people, a small living room furnished with a couch and a desk, a tiny bathroom, and a small bedroom.

The one thing that wasn't small in any way was their love—a love which Sal knew was eternal. Sal placed his copy of the Book of Mormon on the desk in the living room, and looked around at the cozy apartment. *Where would I be if I hadn't studied the Book of Mormon? What would have happened to my relationship with Amy if I hadn't investigated and found out its truthfulness? The Book of Mormon is truly the keystone of Mormonism; its prophets are my teachers and mentors. Now, with my marriage to Amy, it has become my Capstone of Faith.*

Afterward

Sal had seen his father in the sealing room on his wedding day. He couldn't explain it, but see him he had. The manifestation motivated Sal to get his family's temple work done as quickly as possible. Very patiently, with help from Amy and her parents, he taught his mother and sisters the Gospel. The Spirit had already touched their hearts, making it unnecessary to do much convincing. Within months they were baptized.

The excitement of going back to the temple to do the work for his family was as great as that of his own wedding day. Amy and her mother sat on each side of Guadalupe during the endowment. Sal wiped tears from his eyes as he took his father's name for a proxy endowment. Hairs on his neck tingled throughout the session as he felt his father's presence.

Brother Mecham served as proxy for his father in the sealing room. He knelt opposite his mother at the altar while they were sealed in the Celestial covenant of marriage. His mother and father were now married for time and eternity. Teary-eyed, Sal watched as his three little sisters were led into the sealing room. The girls knelt on one end of the altar, he on the other. They placed their hands on the altar, on top of those of his mother and Brother Mecham—who was still proxy for his father. Kneeling around the sacred altar, the family was sealed. They were now an eternal family.